# COPING WITHOUT YOU

### DI SALLY PARKER SERIES
#### BOOK TWELVE

## M A COMLEY

*For my rock, my beautiful mother, who is now watching over me. Dementia sucks. Remembering all the good times we shared together.*

*You took a huge chunk of my heart with you. Love you and will miss you, until we're reunited once more.*

## ALSO BY M A COMLEY

Blind Justice (Novella)
Cruel Justice (Book #1)
Mortal Justice (Novella)
Impeding Justice (Book #2)
Final Justice (Book #3)
Foul Justice (Book #4)
Guaranteed Justice (Book #5)
Ultimate Justice (Book #6)
Virtual Justice (Book #7)
Hostile Justice (Book #8)
Tortured Justice (Book #9)
Rough Justice (Book #10)
Dubious Justice (Book #11)
Calculated Justice (Book #12)
Twisted Justice (Book #13)
Justice at Christmas (Short Story)
Prime Justice (Book #14)
Heroic Justice (Book #15)
Shameful Justice (Book #16)
Immoral Justice (Book #17)
Toxic Justice (Book #18)
Overdue Justice (Book #19)
Unfair Justice (a 10,000 word short story)
Irrational Justice (a 10,000 word short story)

Seeking Justice (a 15,000 word novella)

Caring For Justice (a 24,000 word novella)

Savage Justice ( a 17,000 word novella)

Justice at Christmas #2 (a 15,000 word novella)

Gone in Seconds (Justice Again series #1)

Ultimate Dilemma (Justice Again series #2)

Shot of Silence (Justice Again series #3)

Taste of Fury (Justice Again series #4)

Crying Shame (Justice Again series #5)

To Die For (DI Sam Cobbs #1)

To Silence Them (DI Sam Cobbs #2)

To Make Them Pay (DI Sam Cobbs #3)

To Prove Fatal (DI Sam Cobbs #4)

To Condemn Them (DI Sam Cobbs #5)

To Punish Them (DI Sam Cobbs #6)

To Entice Them (DI Sam Cobbs #7)

To Control Them (DI Sam Cobbs #8)

To Endanger Lives (DI Sam Cobbs #9)

To Hold Responsible (DI Sam Cobbs #10)

To Catch a Killer (DI Sam Cobbs #11)

To Believe The Truth (DI Sam Cobbs #12)

To Blame Them (DI Sam Cobbs #13)

Forever Watching You (DI Miranda Carr thriller)

Wrong Place (DI Sally Parker thriller #1)

No Hiding Place (DI Sally Parker thriller #2)

Cold Case (DI Sally Parker thriller#3)

Deadly Encounter (DI Sally Parker thriller #4)

Lost Innocence (DI Sally Parker thriller #5)

Goodbye My Precious Child (DI Sally Parker #6)

The Missing Wife (DI Sally Parker #7)

Truth or Dare (DI Sally Parker #8)

Where Did She Go? (DI Sally Parker #9)

Sinner (DI Sally Parker #10)

The Good Die Young (DI Sally Parker #11)

Coping Without You (DI Sally Parker #12)

Web of Deceit (DI Sally Parker Novella)

The Missing Children (DI Kayli Bright #1)

Killer On The Run (DI Kayli Bright #2)

Hidden Agenda (DI Kayli Bright #3)

Murderous Betrayal (Kayli Bright #4)

Dying Breath (Kayli Bright #5)

Taken (DI Kayli Bright #6)

The Hostage Takers (DI Kayli Bright Novella)

No Right to Kill (DI Sara Ramsey #1)

Killer Blow (DI Sara Ramsey #2)

The Dead Can't Speak (DI Sara Ramsey #3)

Deluded (DI Sara Ramsey #4)

The Murder Pact (DI Sara Ramsey #5)

Twisted Revenge (DI Sara Ramsey #6)

The Lies She Told (DI Sara Ramsey #7)

For The Love Of… (DI Sara Ramsey #8)

Run for Your Life (DI Sara Ramsey #9)

Cold Mercy (DI Sara Ramsey #10)

Sign of Evil (DI Sara Ramsey #11)

Indefensible (DI Sara Ramsey #12)

Locked Away (DI Sara Ramsey #13)

I Can See You (DI Sara Ramsey #14)

The Kill List (DI Sara Ramsey #15)

Crossing The Line (DI Sara Ramsey #16)

Time to Kill (DI Sara Ramsey #17)

Deadly Passion (DI Sara Ramsey #18)

Son of the Dead (DI Sara Ramsey #19)

Evil Intent (DI Sara Ramsey #20)

The Games People Play (DI Sara Ramsey #21)

Revenge Streak (DI Sara Ramsey #22)

Seeking Retribution (DI Sara Ramsey #23)

I Know The Truth (A Psychological thriller)

She's Gone (A psychological thriller)

Shattered Lives (A psychological thriller)

Evil In Disguise – a novel based on True events

Deadly Act (Hero series novella)

Torn Apart (Hero series #1)

End Result (Hero series #2)

In Plain Sight (Hero Series #3)

Double Jeopardy (Hero Series #4)

Criminal Actions (Hero Series #5)

Regrets Mean Nothing (Hero series #6)

Prowlers (Di Hero Series #7)

Sole Intention (Intention series #1)

Grave Intention (Intention series #2)

Devious Intention (Intention #3)

Cozy mysteries

Murder at the Wedding

Murder at the Hotel

Murder by the Sea

Death on the Coast

Death By Association

Merry Widow (A Lorne Simpkins short story)

It's A Dog's Life (A Lorne Simpkins short story)

A Time To Heal (A Sweet Romance)

A Time For Change (A Sweet Romance)

High Spirits

The Temptation series (Romantic Suspense/New Adult Novellas)

Past Temptation

Lost Temptation

Clever Deception (co-written by Linda S Prather)

Tragic Deception (co-written by Linda S Prather)

Sinful Deception (co-written by Linda S Prather)

ACKNOWLEDGMENTS

Special thanks as always go to @studioenp for their superb cover design expertise.

My heartfelt thanks go to my wonderful editor Emmy and my proofreaders Joseph and Barbara for spotting all the lingering nits.

Thank you also to my amazing ARC Group who help to keep me sane during this process.

To Mary, gone, but never forgotten. I hope you found the peace you were searching for my dear friend. I miss you each and every day.

# PROLOGUE

*Two years before*

THE SESSION HAD GONE BETTER than Christian had expected. Everyone had played their part in making it a success, which was always an absolute bonus in his eyes. It definitely made his life a lot easier when everyone put in a hundred and ten percent effort.

"Thanks for a great class, Christian, it was worth all the sweat and tears." Annabelle flashed her eyelashes and a couple of the other girls groaned behind her.

"I'm glad there was no blood shed, Annabelle. I'll take all the sweat and tears you guys want to put in, if we achieve incredible results such as we have tonight. Enjoy the rest of your evening, everyone."

He collected his personal belongings together and shoved them into his Adidas holdall that had seen better days, then he whizzed around the dance studio, gathering up all the floor mats he'd dotted around to carry out certain exercises during the course of the evening. With everything safely locked away in the storeroom, he switched off the lights and ensured the building was locked up before heading home himself for the evening.

Except, he never made it home, and his wife and daughter haven't laid eyes on him since that evening…

## CHAPTER 1

DI Sally Parker and her partner, DS Lorne Warner, entered the station together after arriving for duty in the same car.

"Thanks again for the lift, Sal. No idea what is wrong with that bloody car of mine now. Tony swears he fixed the fault last week. Don't ask me what it is that has gone wrong this time, but he reckons it's something entirely different."

"Don't worry about it, neighbour, it's not like I had to go out of my way to pick you up, is it?"

They both laughed.

"True enough."

They climbed the stairs to the Cold Case Team's office.

"I wonder what today will bring," Sally said. "No doubt there will be a mountain of post to deal with. I swear it must arrive in my office and breed while it's sitting there, bulging in my tray. I thought running this team would put an end to being snowed under with daily emails and postal queries from head office."

"Think again, and they wonder why the crime rates are on the increase."

Sally opened the outer door to the office and switched on the lights. "It sucks, doesn't it? I bet you're relieved not to be dealing with that side of things any longer."

"I can't deny it, however, if ever you need me to lend you a hand, you only have to ask. Have you heard from Jack lately?"

Jack had been Sally's partner for years but had finally retired from the Force after sustaining a bad injury. However, he hadn't retired altogether, far from it. No, he'd set up business as a private investigator in the area and had, over the past few months, become a thorn in Sally's side, constantly calling her for advice on how he should handle certain cases and also begging for information that could only be found via the police databases. At first, Sally had played along, giving him what he needed, but it was all wearing a tad thin now, which she'd told him on more than one occasion.

"Not for a week or so. Let's hope he's finally got the message that I can't be at his beck and call twenty-four-seven. I love the man to pieces, but let's just say he pushed me to the limits a few months after he started up that confounded business of his. My opinion is that he rushed into it and didn't carry out the necessary research he needed before taking the exam. I told him, even begged him, at one point to dig deep before putting his money into a new business. Did he ever sit down with you and Tony to have a chat? I told him time and time again that you two were the experts on the subject, not me."

"I think he had a five-minute conversation with Tony during that barbecue we had straight after his farewell drinks party. Between you and me, I think he asked a few naïve questions but didn't really listen to the answers."

"That man needs shooting. You know why, don't you? Because he knows, or thinks he knows, that he can count on me to supply him with the answers, as if I haven't got enough stress of my own as it is to deal with around this place. Well, if he's not prepared to help himself, that's it, I'm done with him. He can go whistle the next time he calls on me to assist him."

"That's a bit harsh, especially if he's relying on you to come up with the goods, Sal."

Sally pointed at Lorne. "See, that's just it, he's become reliant on me. What began as a favour has gone way too far, and I've got enough on my plate during a shift here, without adding his shit to the mix. No, I'm adamant about this, he isn't going to like it and will probably call me all the names under the sun, but tough shit, it's about time I put my foot down regarding my *former* partner. He made his bed, it's up to him, and him alone, to deal with the consequences."

As if on cue, Sally's mobile rang. She angled it towards Lorne.

"Speak of the devil," Lorne said and laughed.

Sally jabbed the red button on her screen to end the call. "He can get stuffed. Christ, where's the coffee? I'm in dire need of caffeine to steady the ship now."

"I'll make it and bring it in to you."

"Now that's a great partner. Always willing to put my needs before her own."

Lorne chuckled. "Maybe it's a female trait that some men severely lack."

"Probably. I'm going to make a start on the other dross blighting my life." Sally entered her office and switched on the light. Although it was coming up to nine, it was still a dull and dreary day. "Roll on spring. You can't come quickly enough for me."

Lorne came into the room and caught her looking out at the view of the flat landscape. Norfolk was a lovely part of the world, but what Sally wouldn't give for some stunning mountain scenery right now to brighten her mood.

"Penny for them?" Lorne asked.

"I was just thinking how wonderful it would be to take off and climb a mountain somewhere. You know, stand at the very top and yodel to my heart's content."

"You crack me up," her partner replied.

"I know. A girl can dream, can't she? I guess living in the flattest part of the country has its drawbacks some days. Saying that, I don't think I would swap it and live anywhere else."

"I don't suppose there's any chance of the four of us ever getting away together now that I'm your partner at work."

Sally faced her. "Yeah, not so good, eh? We didn't think that part through very well before you decided to come out of retirement, did we?"

"Never mind. We'll make up for it when we all retire, eh? If the boys ever give up being property developers."

"Can't see that happening anytime soon, can you?"

"Not when everything they seem to touch turns to gold, even in these uncertain times."

"They're to be admired. Mind you, they have my dad to thank for keeping them on the straight and narrow, as well. They're a great team. Right, enough chat, I must get on. Feel free to come and rescue me in an hour or so."

"Will do. Have fun."

"Can you and the team keep trawling through the paperwork needed for the cases that are coming up for trial?"

"Sure, I think we're just about there now."

"Glad to hear it. I bet another case comes our way before the week is out."

"I hope so. There's nothing worse than sitting around here doing sod all, not that it has ever happened, of course."

"We'll see what pans out in the next couple of days. If we

can concentrate on tying everything up regarding the other cases then that can only be a good thing and work in our favour, right?"

"Absolutely. Ah, I hear the rest of the team arriving now. I'll leave you to have your fun."

"Thanks." Sally made her way to her desk and groaned when she saw the pile of brown envelopes awaiting her. Pushing them aside for the time being, she booted up her computer and checked her emails, only to find she had a personal email from a friend of hers, someone she hadn't heard from in a while. She scan-read the email and then picked up her phone. "Kim. How the dickens are you? Long time no hear."

"Hi, Sally. I take it you've read my email?"

"I have. I thought I'd give you a call, so you could tell me more about your friend's dilemma."

"I'm so grateful to you for getting back to me. Poor Zara is beside herself. She's been living on the edge of an abyss for the past couple of years. She saw the documentary that aired last week about your Cold Case Team, and she's been pleading with me ever since to reach out to you."

"Okay, I'm intrigued to hear more. Do you want to meet up for a coffee, rather than discuss it over the phone?"

"That would be amazing. It's been far too long since we caught up."

"I know. I feel guilty for not keeping in touch. I'm sure you appreciate how busy life gets, not just for me, but for all of us."

"Totally. Since I started my business, I haven't had time to even consider taking a holiday."

"How's it going?"

"It was going great until the dreaded pandemic knocked the wind out of our sails. How I kept the bakery going, I'll never know. Still, things appear to be on the up again now. I'll tell you all about it when we meet."

"How are you fixed this morning?"

"I can manage to fit you in at about ten, if you like. Why don't you come here? We might as well make use of the café now it's up and running properly."

"I thought you had a bakery. Ah, I see, you've had to diversify, just like every other business I know."

"You'll see when you get here, it's much more than just a café."

"Can't wait. Okay, I remember where you are. All right if I bring my partner with me? I think you've met Lorne before at a social gathering."

"Of course. She's your partner? I thought she retired from the Force years ago."

"She did. I persuaded her to join my Cold Case Team, and she's been amazing ever since. Jack has moved on to pastures new, so she stepped in and became my partner."

"What a thrill for you both, or is it? It's always dicey working alongside friends and family. I should know, I could throttle my sister, Gemma, sometimes, especially when she lets me down at the last minute at the café. It was her idea to start one up, and I foolishly thought she would enjoy running it for me… never been so wrong in all my life."

"Bugger, that doesn't sound good. Stressful, I should imagine?"

"And some. I'll see you in an hour. That'll give me enough time to get things organised around here, and Sally, thanks for agreeing to see me at such short notice."

"My pleasure. Your email dropped at the right time; you caught my team in between cases. I can't make any promises, but we'll see what we can do for your friend."

"That's music to my ears. See you soon. I'll line up a couple of nice surprises for you and Lorne."

"Nothing too fattening, it's getting harder to shift the excess baggage as I get older."

"Get away with you. A little nibble won't hurt."

"We'll see. We'll be with you in about an hour." Sally hung up and immediately sent a text to Lorne.

BE ready to go in forty-five minutes. We might have a new case on our hands. And yes, I'm feeling lazy and can't be bothered getting off my arse to tell you in person.

SHE INSTANTLY RECEIVED A MESSAGE BACK: *I'll be ready. Promise not to call you a lazy so-and-so when I see you in person.*

SALLY LAUGHED AND TYPED: *It's called saving shoe leather.*

HMM... *I believe you,* Lorne replied.

SALLY KNUCKLED DOWN and got to work emptying her in-tray, even forgoing her coffee, aware of what awaited her when she reached the café. It had been a while since she'd met up with Kim, and she was eager to hear all the gossip surrounding her friend. Kim used to be the girl everyone wanted to hang around with at school and even when they'd gone on to attend university, not that Sally had spent many years at uni once her application to join the police had come through. At first, Kim had been hurt that Sally was deserting her, but Sally had talked her around once she had explained that she'd needed to follow her dreams of righting the wrongs in today's society. They had remained friends for over twenty years, but she hadn't met up with her for around two years now.

Sally collected Lorne on the way out and listened to her hounding her for a clue on where they were going all the way down the stairs. "Patience, dear partner. You'll find out soon enough and you'll thank me in the end, I promise."

"What's that supposed to mean?"

"Christ, it's a surprise, that's all you need to know."

"All right, I'll stop going on if I'm going to benefit from our trip."

Sally grinned.

They parked in a space close to the café. Sally admired the array of savoury pastries and calorie-loaded sweet goods on offer in the window as they walked past. She hooked an arm through Lorne's and steered her through the front door. Inside, they entered a charming, cosy atmosphere. Six pine tables to the right of the area were surrounded by wall-to-wall bookshelves.

"Wow, this is amazing, but what are we doing here?" Lorne asked, her brow furrowed.

"Sally Parker, as I live and breathe. Look at you. Obviously, marriage the second time around agrees with you," Kim shouted from behind the counter. She lifted the flap and ran towards Sally with her arms outstretched. "It's been far too long. I've missed seeing you, Parker."

Unexpected tears misted Sally's eyes. "Now don't start. You know how much I hate blubbering in public. You remember Lorne, don't you?"

"Of course I do. How are you, Lorne? I was surprised to learn that you're now this one's partner. I'm sure you're going to make a really successful team. I remember how pig-headed Ms Parker can be."

"Oi, you. I am in the room, and furthermore, I dispute that. Not pig-headed, more confident about what's going on in my head and putting my point across."

Kim jabbed a thumb in Sally's direction. "Get her. What would you call it, Lorne?"

"Oh heck, please don't get me involved, I happen to like my job. If I tick Sally off saying the wrong thing, my life won't be worth living."

Kim chuckled. "Fair enough. You've caught us during a quiet spell. Why don't you take a seat and I'll grab some cakes? I won't be offended if you reject them, given the time of day."

Sally snorted and leaned towards Lorne. "Believe that and you'll believe anything."

Kim went back to the counter laughing her socks off.

"You two still have a great rapport with each other, even though you haven't seen each other for a while," Lorne pointed out.

"I suppose good friends always pick up where they left off. It's always been the same with us, hasn't it?"

"You're right. Oh God, I think I've died and gone to Heaven," Lorne whispered.

Sally spun around, and her eyes widened at the sight of a double-layered cake stand full of delicious goodies. "Oh my. What's that saying? A moment on the lips means a lifetime on the hips."

"But how can you resist this sumptuous offering?" Kim said. She placed the stand on the table closest to them. "Tea or coffee?"

"Two coffees, white, one sugar, please, Kim," Sally answered for both of them. "Crikey, you've definitely outdone yourself here. I think we're going to need a doggy bag."

"It can be arranged. See how far you can get while I sort out the drinks. I won't be long." Kim left them both dumbstruck, grappling for words.

"Don't think of the calories, we'll enrol in the gym down the road from the station if we need to. This is too good to miss out on," Sally said.

She gestured for Lorne to take a seat, and they both tucked into a cream horn, half coated in chocolate.

"This is to die for," Lorne moaned.

"Isn't it?" Sally agreed.

Kim arrived with the coffees and slid them across the table. "Well? What do you think?"

"Like you have to ask. It's bloody obvious how much we're enjoying them." Sally reached for a serviette and wiped a spot of cream from her chin.

"I'm glad you like them. Do you want to discuss my friend's problem now, or would you rather leave it until you've finished?"

"If you can ignore the moans of pleasure, then feel free to go ahead," Sally replied.

"And who is going to take notes?" Lorne mumbled, sounding put out.

"Oops, I forgot about that. Okay, maybe we should delay it for a second or two."

Kim smiled. "I can give you the gist of it, can't I? We can revisit the facts if you need to take notes later, how's that?"

Despite complaining, Lorne removed her notebook from her pocket and poised her pen whilst still managing to fill her face with cream cakes. "I'm ready."

"Where there's a will, eh?" Sally laughed. "Why don't you start from the beginning, Kim?"

With one eye on the girl holding the fort behind the

counter, filling up the cabinets with fresh supplies, Kim sighed and said, "Just over two years ago, Zara's husband went missing. They ran a dance studio together and they took it in turns to hold evening classes during the week, ensuring that their daughter, Mila, always had at least one parent at home with her."

"How old was the daughter?"

"She's sixteen now, so she would have been fourteen at the time. Lovely girl, they've never had any issues with her. She's very respectful to her elders and absolutely adores her parents."

"It sounds like they were the ideal family, or were they?"

"Yes, Zara and Christian always loved being with each other. They went on weekend jaunts away to the seaside throughout the UK and even took mini-breaks away to France and Holland. They worked hard and felt they had earnt the right to be together as a family, enjoying the benefits of all their hard work."

"Quite right, and why not? I think a lot of people who are self-employed could learn from them. Everyone needs a break now and again, if only to recharge their batteries."

Kim nodded and raised an eyebrow. "I'll take that piece of advice on board the next time I come down here on a Sunday to get an urgent order filled or to file my tax returns."

Sally grinned. "You were saying? Can you tell us what led up to him going missing?"

"It was Christian's turn to hold the evening class that night. As far as Zara knew, everything had gone as normal and he had locked up and driven home, except, he never made it. Poof, it was like he vanished into thin air. As if a tornado had struck and sucked him in."

"And Zara hasn't heard a word from him since? Or from anyone else, relating to his disappearance?"

"Nothing, absolutely zilch. She's at a loss to know what

happened to him, and it's been driving her crazy since he left. Like I said before, she saw you on that documentary the other night and begged me to ask you if there was any hope of you revisiting the case."

"Revisiting the case? Are you telling me the police were involved at the time of his disappearance?"

"Yes. I don't wish to cast aspersions, but the officer in charge was as useless as a chocolate teapot."

"Two years ago... hmm... we can't be talking about DI Falkirk here, can we?"

"I don't think that was his name. I know Zara said he was a young officer. He took the facts down from her, and that was basically the last she heard from him. He told her that he would contact her if any news came to light. Zara presumed that would happen and didn't push the point."

*Strange... why wouldn't she push the point?* Sally placed the cake she was nibbling back on her plate and sighed. "People have a genuine right to know what's going on with an investigation. It sickens me when I hear that people have been let down by the police; it should never happen, ever. That's what we're here for, to serve the public, not treat people as if they're an inconvenience. Sometimes it takes a lot of courage for people to seek out our help, only to be disregarded at the first hurdle. Sorry, I'll get off my soapbox now. As you can tell, this kind of behaviour incenses me beyond words."

Kim covered Sally's hand with her own. "You always did have a good heart. Maybe it's a male thing. Perhaps women tend to be more compassionate on the whole?"

Lorne nodded. "I think you've hit the nail on the head there, Kim. I've dealt with some pretty inconsiderate male colleagues over the years—granted, not closely—but they were there, nevertheless. You only have to see the reports coming out these days about the state the Met Police is in... still, the less we say about that the better. Let's just say I resigned more times over the years than I would have done if my senior officer had been a female."

"Really? Wow, Lorne. That's a bloody eye-opener. What a frigging world we live in if we can't rely on the police, especially male officers."

Sally held her hands up. "Hey, let's not blow this up out of all proportion. Every business, and career, throughout the world has had issues along these lines, I'm guessing since the prehistoric times. In my opinion, a serving officer, whether they are male or female, should never treat someone seeking help with contempt. When we get back to the station, we'll need to look up the file and do the necessary digging ourselves into why the officer in question treated Zara so appallingly."

"Oh Christ, don't tell me I've opened a can of worms, got someone in trouble about this?" Kim said. She reached for an iced finger and nibbled on it. "They're just too tempting, aren't they?"

"They are, and no, you haven't dropped someone in it. If you hadn't told us, the information would have come to light eventually. Anyway, we'll deal with that side of things later. So, what did Zara do when she found out Christian had gone missing?"

"The usual, sat up all night, called all her friends and family to see if they had heard from him then, as time progressed, she and her friends contacted the hospitals in the area. They even went out there, day and night, taking it in shifts, to search for him. But it all proved to be pointless. No one had seen him, not even a glimpse of him. We began to wonder if he'd been kidnapped, and Zara waited by the phone for weeks, willing a kidnapper to contact her, to do a deal with them in exchange for money. Nothing like that ever happened. I suppose that's the frustrating part. She's been left to cope without a single word from anyone. Putting myself in her shoes, she must have been going out of her mind for the past two years."

"Has her health suffered?" Sally asked.

Kim's eyes watered. "Yes, definitely. She's a shadow of her former self. She always had the perfect figure, she's a dancer for goodness' sake, but now, she's painfully thin. I'd even call her anorexic. She's lost clumps of hair, her eyes are sunken. Between you and me, she's nothing more than a walking skeleton."

The three of them glanced at the cakes and sat back.

"Maybe you should take her a batch of cakes round," Lorne suggested.

"Believe me, I've tried. She always leaves them in the kitchen and tells me that she'll eat them later. She never does."

"That poor woman," Sally said. "But, while we can all feel sorry for her, I'm really not sure what we can do to help, Kim, and yes, that's me being blunt and to the point."

"Oh no, don't say that, Sal. I felt sure you'd be able to help her. Won't you at least meet with her? She's been let down so much in the past by the police…"

"That's it, make me feel guilty," Sally replied. "What do you think, Lorne?"

"I think we owe it to Zara to at least take a cursory look over her case. What harm can it do, Sally?"

She tipped her head back and studied the ceiling that was dotted with plastic stars. "Out of interest, what are they for?"

Kim glanced up. "A failed experiment. I thought they'd add a bit of sparkle when the shop was empty, entice the punters as they walked past, that sort of thing."

"And they don't, I take it?"

"Nope. I'll try anything if it means bringing in more business. You can see how quiet we are. I'm not saying it's like this all the time, it's not, but like any business, we have our dull moments. That aside, please won't you reconsider, Sally? She's a desperate woman. If she were sitting here now, I'm telling you, your heart would go out to her."

"I have no doubt about that, hon. But when we take on a case, there has to be an inkling that we're going to find the person we're searching for. In Christian's case, if he's not been seen or heard from since he went missing and there are no leads for us to track…" Sally stopped talking after she noticed the way Lorne was staring at her. "Don't you start."

Lorne slapped a hand to her chest. "Moi? What have I said?"

"You don't have to actually say anything. I can tell what you're thinking just by looking at you."

Lorne grinned and shrugged. "Perhaps that's your guilty conscience pricking you."

"Who asked for your opinion?" Sally bit back jokingly. "All right, between you, you've beaten me into submission. When can we meet Zara?"

Kim glanced nervously at the girl behind the counter and lowered her voice, "She's not the most reliable member of staff I've got, so there's no way I can leave her to run the shop for me, and it's going to start getting busy soon, otherwise I'd volunteer to take you round there."

"Do you think she'd rather have you there when we visit her?" Sally asked.

"Maybe not, it's hard to tell. If you go alone, you will promise to treat her gently and with compassion, won't you?"

Sally frowned. "What do you take me for? Of course I will! Any friend of yours is a friend of mine. Maybe you should give her a call first, ask her if she's up to seeing us today."

"Today?" Kim said, aghast. "As in right now?"

"The sooner the better by the sounds of it. Give her a call, will you? We can shoot around there now, rather than delay things further. Sounds like the woman deserves a break, and it's not like we're inundated with cases at the moment."

Kim tipped her chair back as she stood and hugged Sally, planting kisses all over her face. "Thank you, thank you, thank you. You have no idea how much this means to me."

Sally swiped a hand in front of her. "I don't have to be a genius to figure that out. But you're going to need to keep your emotions in check, for now at least. I've only said I'll consider the case. If there's nothing there for us to go on, then there's really little we can do to help."

"I'll get my phone. Promise me you'll give her a chance, Sal."

"I will." Sally glanced over her shoulder, checking the coast was clear before she whispered to Lorne, "Are we doing the right thing here?"

"What harm can it do? The woman is obviously desperate to find her husband. I feel gutted that yet another male officer has let her down."

"Me, too. More than gutted, I'm bloody livid. I believe it would be remiss of us not to take a fleeting peek at the case."

"Want me to get a member of the team to pull the file up for us?"

"Great idea. We might as well have everything to hand for when we return."

Lorne sank her teeth into another mini cake, this time a pink macaroon, and then placed the call. "Hi, Joanna, it's Lorne. We're considering taking on another cold case but could do with getting all the background information sorted for when we return."

"Okay, I can see what I can find. What's the name, Lorne?"

"Christian… shit, hang on." She covered the phone and said, "Do we know Zara's surname?"

"I don't think Kim's mentioned it yet. I'll ask." Sally left her seat and walked over to the counter. "Kim, what's Zara's surname?"

"Sorry, I should have told you, it's Starr, with two R's."

"Thanks." She returned to her seat. "Starr... S-t-a-r-r."

Lorne repeated the information to Joanna. "See what you can find. We're going to pay the wife a visit now."

"Leave it with me."

Lorne ended the call. "It's better to get the ball rolling as early as possible."

"I agree."

Kim rejoined them after they had tucked into yet another cake. "I've brought a couple of boxes with me, feel free to load them up."

"Thanks," Sally said. She took one of the boxes and started filling it. "Did you ring Zara?"

"I did. She's expecting you. She broke down when I said you were heading over there to see her. You will be gentle with her, won't you?"

"I'm not in the habit of repeating myself, of course we will. I'm shocked you would think otherwise. Is it far?"

"No, about ten minutes from here. I quite often call in on my way home from work to see her, not that she's ever up to receiving visitors. It's Mila I feel sorry for. She rarely gets out to socialise with her friends, she's always stuck at home in the evening with her mother."

"That's a shame. Don't worry, you have my word that if we can help, we will. These are all delicious, Kim, thanks so much. Do you want us to pay for them?"

Kim frowned and crossed her arms. "I'm going to ignore that question. Call it a token of my appreciation for going to see Zara. She's such a wonderful lady who deserves to be treated better by the police. I know you won't let me down, Sally. It was lovely to see you again, both of you."

"I'll give you a call later to let you know how we've got on and if we're considering taking the case on or not."

Kim held up her crossed fingers. "Thanks, Sally. You're a true friend. Maybe we can go out for dinner one night?"

"Or you could come over for one of Simon's notorious barbecues. Lorne and her husband, Tony, are always there. They bought the house next door to us."

"That's brilliant. Yes, I'd love to come. I'm on my own nowadays. Totally fed up with being used by fellas. The ones I've dated recently seem to think I'm rolling in it, just because I run my own business. Ha, not these days, especially with costs escalating all the time. Anyway, enough about me. Good luck with Zara. Here's her address." She handed Sally a slip of paper.

"Take care of yourself. I'll call you later. What about this evening, will that be better for you?"

"That would be perfect."

Sally and Kim hugged, and Lorne collected the boxes from the table.

"Thanks for the cakes, they're all amazing, Kim. Hope to catch up with you soon."

"Spread the word, I'll be forever grateful."

Sally and Lorne left the café and crossed the road to the car. Sally put the cakes in a crate in the boot to prevent them from sliding around during the journey.

Back in the car, she said, "It was lovely catching up with Kim. I'm sorry her business isn't doing better."

"We'll have to put a note up in the station for the staff."

"Now that's an excellent idea." Sally put the address into the satnav and set off.

Ten minutes later, they pulled up outside a small end-of-terrace house in Caldercott Street, Dereham.

"Let's see what Zara has to say."

Lorne dipped her head and looked up at the house. "It's a bit run-down."

"I was thinking the same. Hey, we shouldn't judge a book by its cover."

They left the car, and Sally rang the bell. There were no front gardens to the properties on this side of the road. She fixed a smile in place, and when the door opened to reveal Zara, she had to dig deep not to show any reaction to the woman's godawful appearance.

"Hi, Zara? I'm DI Sally Parker, and this is my partner, DS Lorne Warner."

"Oh yes, Kim told me to expect you. Please come in. You'll have to excuse the mess, I don't have many visitors."

"Don't worry, we promise not to judge."

They followed Zara into a warm and cosy lounge that was very tidy, with nothing noticeable out of place.

"This is lovely, have you been here long?" Sally asked.

"About two years. After Christian…" Zara paused to inhale and exhale a couple of breaths and then continued, "After my husband went missing, I found it impossible keeping up with the bills at the last house. I bit the bullet and downsized, doing my best to avoid getting into financial difficulties with Mila around."

"That's your daughter, yes?"

"That's right. Sorry, take a seat. Can I get you a drink?"

"Not for us. Kim fed and watered us well before we ventured over here."

Sally and Lorne sat on the sofa while Zara lowered herself gingerly into a reclining chair by the gas fire.

"She's such a good friend, and her cakes are out of this world. I wish I had the appetite I once had but I just haven't got one these days, as you can probably tell."

"Sorry to ask such a personal question, but are you ill?" Sally asked tentatively.

"Sick of life, I'd guess you'd call it. I miss my husband dearly. I know I have my daughter, but I fear if I didn't have her, I wouldn't be here today."

"I'm sorry to hear that, Zara. Have you thought about having counselling?"

"No, I don't believe in it. I have good friends and neighbours; they keep me going most of the time. Kim is at the top of the list. She's been so kind to me and my daughter over the past two years."

"She's one of the best. I've known Kim since our school days."

"She speaks highly of you, too. She's been a massive support to me, long before Christian went missing. Not everyone would go out of their way to make sure a friend is coping, not when they run a successful business like she does, and that was before she opened up the coffee shop. I think she struggles finding decent staff. I've often thought about volunteering in the café, just to keep my mind active and not constantly thinking about what might have happened to Christian. It's all-consuming when someone disappears from your life, especially when we had a great marriage. I sit here wondering if that truly was the case."

"And have you come to any conclusion?" Sally asked.

"No. Laughter filled our home every day. That's all people need for a happy and content life, isn't it?"

"Absolutely. Are you saying there were never any problems within your marriage?"

"Not that I can think of." Her head dropped, and she picked at a loose piece of cotton hanging from her top.

"Zara? I'm getting the impression that you're not being completely honest with us."

She glanced up, and her gaze flitted between them, and then the tears flowed down her colourless cheeks. "I... umm... I..."

Even though Sally's heart went out to the woman, she needed to know that she could trust what Zara was telling them. "Zara, if you hold back any information from us at this stage then we might as well call it a day now and leave."

"I'm sorry. I'm such a mess. My life imploded the day he went missing, but that was nothing compared to what occurred in the weeks afterwards."

"Care to enlighten us?" Sally asked.

Lorne withdrew her notebook and flipped it open to a new page.

"Zara, you need to tell us. To confide in us. We're not here to judge you, we won't think badly of you."

"When I told the policeman dealing with the case, I never saw him again. I'm scared the same thing will happen with you."

"It won't, I promise. I'll be honest with you, we haven't had a chance to go over your case, so we're going into this totally blind. You need to tell us *everything*."

"A few days after Christian disappeared, the debts started rolling in. I was oblivious to the loans he had taken out over the years. We had a successful dance studio, and he borrowed against it, without my knowledge."

"And you have no idea where the money went, what it was used for?"

"I trusted him. Left all the finances to him. He dealt with the accounts while I organised the classes and the frequent charity events we often put on. I know we used to take off for weekends, here, there and everywhere, but I thought we had the money to pay for our extravagant behaviour. Clearly, I was mistaken."

Sally inclined her head and asked, "How much are we talking about here?"

Zara paused for a moment or two and then said. "Eighty grand. He took out two loans of forty thousand each."

"Ouch, that must have been hard to deal with."

"It tore me apart. As soon as I mentioned it to the police officer in charge of the case, that was it, he walked away, and I never laid eyes on him again. He didn't give me a reason for ditching me either. I was too stunned to chase it up or to put in a complaint. What was the point? I gave him the facts, everything I knew, and that was the outcome."

"It's a difficult one. He probably felt that nothing sinister had happened to your husband, that Christian simply ran off before the debts surfaced and spoilt things between you."

"Oh my, that thought never occurred to me. So, you believe he's out there somewhere, still racking up debts, probably in my name?"

Sally raised a finger. "Not necessarily. The last thing I want to do is cause you any extra stress."

"Is there any way you can find out for me? Search your systems to see if he's still asking for money from these companies without them getting in touch with me before they hand over the funds?"

"Sadly not."

She covered her face with her hands and sobbed. "How is this allowed to happen? Why wouldn't these firms get in touch with me?"

"Because the whole system needs a good shake-up. My friend's husband forged her signature to extend the mortgage without her knowledge. It wasn't until she discovered a letter in one of his jacket pockets that she knew anything about it."

"That's terrible. So, you think there would have been letters sent to me from the loan companies and he probably intercepted them, is that it?"

"Maybe. Had you had any dealings with the companies in the past?"

"No, I'd never heard of them before, that's why it came as

a total shock to me. Why, why, why did I trust him with all the finances?"

"Please don't punish yourself, you weren't to know. There are some devious people out there who get up to all sorts behind their partner's back. Regrettably, you're not alone, and it happens all too frequently."

She stopped crying long enough to ask, "Will you help me?"

"The honest truth is, I'm not sure. It's not generally something we deal with as a department. I'm going to need to have a word with my DCI first, see if he'll give me the go-ahead to take the case on. *If* Christian is still alive, is there anywhere he's likely to be? Either around here or anywhere else in the country perhaps? By that I mean, did he have a special place he loved to visit?"

"Dozens of places, from Scotland to Cornwall and anywhere in between. I'd be jotting down the names of whole areas he adored visiting for weeks."

"Maybe a few of the more popular locations you visited, as a couple?"

"I can try. Let me get a pen and paper." She rose unsteadily and left the room.

"What do you think?" Lorne whispered once the door had shut.

"Apart from him being a grade-one tosspot? I'm sickened by what he's done to her, if he's done it, but I don't think we can help her, not as things stand. We're aware of the statistics of people going missing just to avoid the debts they've created for their family. You ask any debt company, and I bet a high percentage of their cases are related to the same thing."

"It's a worrying trend, but like you say, there's nothing really we can do about it, is there?"

The door opened again before Sally could respond. She

shrugged at Lorne and then rose from her chair when Zara toppled slightly as she walked past.

"Are you all right?"

"I'll be fine, once I'm sitting down again. I'm prone to dizzy spells. I have a very low blood pressure."

"What has the doctor advised you to do, going forward?" Sally eased her into her chair and then returned to her seat.

"He's told me to eat more, it's the only way I'm going to cure myself. Which is easier said than done. As soon as I put food in my mouth and swallow, my stomach rejects it. I'm really not sure what I can do to combat that, do you?"

"No, sorry. I would suggest going to your surgery, sitting in the waiting room until your doctor offers you better advice or at least sends you for further tests at the hospital."

"I might try that, if I have the energy to get out of the house. You've seen what happens to me when I leave the room, let alone going through all the rigmarole of getting ready to go out and then walking to the bus stop to get a bus into town."

"Maybe a friend could take you. Not Kim, as she's probably too busy to help you during surgery hours. What about another friend? Could they help?"

"They're a little short on the ground right now. Most of them gave up on me once the weight started dropping off. None of this is intentional, I can assure you. I wouldn't put Mila through all this shit if I could help it. But if I can't eat, then what am I to do?"

"Why don't we drop you off at the hospital ourselves? We could take you to A and E, make them assess you there."

"That's very kind of you, but then what would Mila do without me?"

*She won't have a choice soon. Kim was right, you're a walking skeleton and in desperate need of help.*

"How old is Mila?" Sally knew the answer as Kim had

already told her, but she preferred to hear the facts from Zara herself.

She smiled and said softly, "She's just celebrated her sixteenth birthday."

"Okay, in that case, she's more than capable of fending for herself, wouldn't you agree?"

"But she's used to coming home to find me here. It'll worry her if I'm out when she gets home."

Sally cocked an eyebrow. "You're in a critical state, health wise, even we can see that, and we're not medically trained. Put it this way, if you don't get treated, it's only going to be a matter of time before you become gravely ill, and what use will you be to your daughter then?"

"I've thought about that, and I still can't bring myself to seek the help I need. It's the demons going on in my head that I have trouble fighting. They battle daily. The gist of it is that they're punishing me for driving Christian away. I didn't, not knowingly. Maybe I did it without realising what was going on."

"My advice would be to set all of that aside for now and concentrate on the one thing that truly matters… your health and you getting better. There's only so long a body can go on without food, and if you'll forgive me saying this, truthfully, I don't think you've got long left."

Lorne cleared her throat beside her.

Sally kicked herself for being overly frank with the woman. Maybe it was a case of being cruel to be kind.

"I know what you're saying is true, but what's the point in going on without him?"

"Are you kidding me? After what he's done to you? The loans weren't taken out against your name by mistake, it was intentional fraud. You have to fight this, retain your strength, if only for Mila's sake, Zara. What would she do without you? We all have our burdens to overcome during our time on this earth, some far more challenging than others, but overcome them we must, especially when there are younger members of our families relying on us. Can you imagine the trauma and guilt Mila would probably go through if anything were to happen to you?"

"I know. Don't you think I've considered that? But what use am I to anyone in this state?"

"Then do something about it. I'm not usually this outspoken, especially with someone I've only just met, but it would be remiss of me not to speak out and try to get you the help you need. Think of how Mila would feel losing you, after living the last couple of years without knowing where her father is."

Zara sobbed again. Sally realised she was coming down heavily on the woman, but she felt it was for her own good. She could only imagine what her internal organs were going through. In her opinion, they'd be shutting down pretty soon if the woman persisted to think that she didn't need help.

Sally got to her feet and held out a hand. "Come on, we'll get you to the hospital now. You'll probably be home before Mila gets back anyway."

"I can't… I won't be able to look the doctor in the eye. They'll think I'm crazy and probably lock me up because of mental health issues."

Sally smiled, but inside she totally agreed that would probably be a necessary outcome. She felt sickened to think that Zara's own surgery hadn't realised what was going on, long before it had got to this stage. "We'll leave a note for Mila, unless she has a mobile. Does she?"

"Yes, but I'd rather not worry her. I'll scribble down a few words and leave it by the front door for her."

"You're doing the right thing, Zara. We need to get you the help you need to continue with your battle. Don't give up, because that's what you've been doing, whether you realise it or not."

"I think that's beginning to sink in now. I'm sorry. I never meant things to go this far."

Sally smiled. "The first step to your recovery is admitting you need help in the first place. Come on, let me help you."

It was a struggle for Zara to get to her feet this time. Obviously, her body had used far too much energy the last time she'd left the room.

Zara smiled and whispered a thank you. "Here's the note. I feel bad deserting her like this."

"You're not deserting her, you're finding the help you need that I'm sure is going to improve Mila's life as well as your own. Once we have you settled, then we'll make a start on the investigation."

"What? I thought you said you wouldn't be able to help me?"

"It would be wrong of us not to at least try. I'm still going to need to run it past my senior officer when I get back to the station, but that's the least of our worries. Getting you sorted is at the top of our list right now."

"Thank you, I have no other words. Maybe they'll come later."

Lorne helped Zara to stand while Sally slipped Zara's shoes on and then assisted her to put her jacket on. "All done. How are you feeling now?"

"Weak, as if I'm going to pass out at any moment."

"Hang in there. We'll be at the hospital in a jiffy."

Actually, Norwich hospital was around thirty minutes away.

"I can't thank you enough for putting yourselves out for me like this."

"All in a day's work."

## CHAPTER 2

They arrived at the A & E department within twenty-five minutes. Lorne and Sally assisted a reluctant Zara out of the car and through the main door. Sally gave the receptionist all the relevant information concerning Zara and her condition and, after taking a look at Zara the receptionist immediately pushed a buzzer. A porter arrived with a stretcher, Zara was seen straight away.

Sally and Lorne remained outside the room in triage while the doctor carried out her assessment. She joined them after she'd spent fifteen minutes with Zara.

Sally jumped to her feet and asked, "How is she, Doctor?"

"Not in a good state. Why did you leave it so long to seek help?"

"Nothing to do with us. We only met the woman about an hour ago. It was obvious she needed urgent medical care, hence us bringing her here."

"I'm sorry, I wasn't aware of the facts. I think Zara is going to have to be admitted. We'll put her on a drip and see how she goes with that. She'll also need to undergo a psych assessment; there's a possibility they might section her. I can't see it coming to that, but I'd rather warn you, just to be on the safe side. Who are you if you're not friends of Zara's?"

Sally produced her ID. "We're police officers. As I've previously stated, we only met the poor woman about an hour ago. She's been through a traumatic couple of years. Her husband went missing, and she's struggled to cope with the emotional turmoil she has been thrown into."

"I see. Okay, I apologise for jumping the gun. She's very lucky to still be alive. Another few days at the most, and her organs would have started shutting down. Who knows what damage has been caused already?"

"Just do your best for her, Doctor, that's all we can ask."

"Oh, we will, don't worry. You're free to see her if you want. I'll get on and make the necessary arrangements for her admittance. Thank you for insisting that she should visit us today. You made the right decision, forcing her to come."

"Glad to hear it. Thank you for seeing her so promptly."

The doctor set off up the corridor.

"What are we going to do?" Lorne asked.

"We'll get her settled and then go back to the station. I want to read through the file, get a feel for what went on when Christian was first reported missing."

"What's your take on it?"

"That he's done a runner, set up home elsewhere, maybe with another woman. That's what is concerning me, that he might be out there, sowing his oats, deceiving yet another, dare I say it, gullible woman."

"And what if we've got this all wrong? Doing him an injustice?"

"Don't forget the debt and fraud he left her with."

"Maybe that happened because of the pressure he was under."

Sally pondered her partner's words for a while and nodded. "Only time will tell. Let's put this to one side for now, see how Zara is." She entered the room.

Zara smiled tentatively at them. It was then that Sally noticed how discoloured her teeth were. She resisted the temptation to shudder with revulsion under the woman's watchful gaze.

*What a shame that she's got into such a state. What about Mila? Didn't she come into the equation?*

"How are you feeling about what lies ahead of you?"

"Like I no longer have a say in what goes on in my life."

"Nonsense, of course you do."

"There's talk of me being sectioned. That's the last thing I wanted or need."

Sally wagged her finger, sensing the woman was going to try to leave the hospital before she gave the nursing staff the opportunity to help her. "Please, give them a chance. If you cooperate and show a willingness to accept medical treatment to aid your recovery, then I'm sure you'll be out of here soon. If, on the other hand, you rebel and insist on leaving, then I fear they might wash their hands of you altogether. You wouldn't want that, not after you've plucked up the courage to come here, seeking help today, would you?"

Zara sighed and clenched her fists beside her on the bed. "All this is such a mess. To think, when I was married, and before Christian went missing, I was what you'd class as a *normal* person. I detest seeing what I've become but I never envisaged my life imploding."

"We know. Don't worry, we're here to support you. We're not about to walk away and leave you high and dry. You're going to need to trust us."

"I do. I know I've only known you a little while, but I do trust you. You have kind faces, that's always meant a lot to me."

Sally chuckled. "We have our moments, I can assure you. Lorne here has dealt with the vilest of criminals, working for the Met in London."

"Really? That must have been a tough area to police, especially for a woman."

"It was, at times. But it was my job. I couldn't hide under a stone, no woman can, not if they're determined to change things for the better in the Force these days."

Zara nodded, and her smile dropped. "What will I do about Mila?"

"What about your family? Can they step in and keep an eye on her for a few days?"

"We've not really spoken for a while. They got fed up with me always going on about Christian and they loathed the area I moved to. I tried to tell them it was out of necessity rather than choice, but they couldn't understand my reasoning at all."

Sally narrowed her eyes and asked, "Really? They weren't prepared to stand by you when your husband walked out on you?"

She shook her head. "I don't think they believed me about the debts. I was mortified as it was and couldn't stand the thought of them criticising me for trusting him."

"Why would they criticise you? Didn't they get on with your husband?"

"Yes, sorry, I didn't mean it to come across as though things were wrong between them. It's pride showing its head, I suppose. My parents have always been so close, they knew everything there was to know about each other's finances, and I guess I felt guilty for allowing myself to be deceived. In my defence, I was running a very successful business at the time so was easily distracted."

"It's okay. If you jot down their numbers, we can call them during the journey back to Dereham."

"What will you tell them?"

"That you're exhausted and need complete rest for a week or so."

"Please tell them not to visit, only to care for my daughter. I'm too ashamed for them to see me like this."

"We'll try and get the point across as succinctly as possible, but if they really care about you, I suspect they'll be very concerned and desperate to see you."

"Maybe, I can't say either way. But I'd rather they didn't see me in this state."

"You have my word that we'll do our best. Who would you rather we call, your parents?"

"Yes, either my mother or my sister... on second thoughts, she's at work full-time whereas my parents are retired and will be able to watch out for Mila better. Sorry, I'm going on longer than should be necessary and not sticking to the point. It just shows how nervous I am about what lies ahead of me, of us, now that I'm in here and you've promised to revisit my case."

"Truly, you're in the best place possible for your health, and there's no need for you to feel apprehensive about our involvement. We'll read the file and see what the officer in charge of your case has to say for himself, if he's still around."

"Thank you for caring, even if the investigation grinds to a halt before it has a chance to get off the ground."

"You're welcome. Now, we're going to leave you to get some much-needed rest, and stop worrying about Mila, promise me?"

"I'm sure she'll be fine with my parents, at least I hope she will be."

Sally patted the back of Zara's scrawny hand and smiled. "Take care of yourself." She wanted to add that Zara would be no good to anyone dead but swallowed down the words.

"See you soon, try not to worry too much," Lorne said.

Sally and Lorne left the room. Sally closed the door and gave Zara one last reassuring smile through the glass pane, but Zara was facing the opposite way. She was staring at the top of the trees visible in the window on the other side of the room.

"Do you think she's going to be all right?" Lorne asked on their rapid walk back to the car.

"I think everyone on the team is going to need to keep their fingers crossed to give her the best chance of pulling through. I suppose it depends on what damage has already been done to her organs as to whether there will be any lasting effects on her recovery."

"I wonder how Mila is going to take the news about her mum finally receiving treatment and also about staying with her grandparents, knowing that they don't get along, if we get through to them."

"Hopefully they'll pick up where they left off and the family will make the effort needed to put things right between them. We'll soon find out." As they neared the car, Sally made the call to Zara's parents. "Hello, sorry to trouble you, is that Amy Walters?"

"That's right. Who wants to know?" The woman sounded understandably wary.

"Hi, I'm Detective Inspector Sally Parker from the Norfolk Constabulary."

"Oh dear. Is something wrong? Is it either of my daughters? Or is it my son, Perry? Please tell me, don't keep me waiting."

"Yes, I'm afraid your daughter, Zara, has been admitted to hospital."

"No! Leslie, Leslie, it's Zara, she's in hospital. Stop what you're doing, we need to go and see her."

"Mrs Walters, please, don't come to the hospital. Zara is fine, she's just exhausted. She needs a few days' rest to recover, and she'll be well enough to go home."

"I don't understand. Exhausted, why? And where's my granddaughter, Mila? Is she all right? Hasn't Zara been taking care of her?"

"Yes, please don't be alarmed. Zara is in the right place now, being cared for by professionals. Actually, Mila is the reason I'm ringing you. Zara suggested I give you a call to see if you'd kindly look after your granddaughter for a few days while Zara is incapacitated."

"Of course we will, that goes without saying. Where is Mila now? Oh wait, she's still at school I should imagine, isn't she?"

"That's right. She's not aware of her mother being in hospital. Is there any chance you can either pick her up or be there at the house when she gets home? Obviously, she'll need to pack a bag before she can come and stay with you."

"What's going on?" a male voice said in the background.

Sally waited patiently while Amy Walters recapped what had happened and what was expected of them.

"Yes, we've got her number. I won't call her yet, I'll leave it until about half an hour before she leaves school. I'm not sure what the school policy is about them having phone calls during the day. Maybe I should ring the school instead?"

"That might be a better idea. Mila is bound to be extremely worried about her mother, so please do your best to reassure her that she's doing okay and getting the help she needs for now."

"Yes, I will. I take it you're aware there has been a strain on our relationship with our daughter for a while?"

"She did mention it. It's not my place to interfere, but I will tell you it took immense courage for Zara to reach out to you. Maybe you can take that into consideration going forward?"

"Yes, we will. If only she hadn't moved to that dreadful area, we would still be in regular contact with them today and she wouldn't be in the situation she finds herself in now."

"Perhaps. Don't be too hard on your daughter. I think once she's better and is released from the hospital, maybe it would be better if you all sat down and had a chat."

"We've always been here for her. Probably the fact that we have a stubborn streak running through each and every one of us works against us at times."

"She's going to need her family around her over the coming days and weeks."

"We'll be there. Sorry if I sound a little confused, but why are the police involved?"

"She's reached out to us to have another look at her case."

"Her case? Christian's disappearance? After all this time? Has something come to light? Has he been seen?"

"Yes, her husband's disappearance, and no, he hasn't been seen. We're going to head back to the station now. I need to read the original file, see what that contains; however, I will need to have a word with all her family and friends in the near future. I'll be able to fill you in more once things become clearer."

"I see. Well, all this has come as a shock to me. We'll be happy to welcome Mila with open arms, there's no need for you to be worried about that."

"I felt sure you would."

"Why do you say that? Did Zara have any doubts?"

"Let's just say she was apprehensive about who would watch out for her daughter and leave it there, shall we?"

"I want to assure you that even though we have fallen out recently, we have never stopped loving our daughter. Some families might cut each other out of their lives, but not us. Stubbornness can be a terrible trait to combat for all concerned. But combat we must, for all our sakes by the sound of it. Can you tell me more about my daughter's condition?"

"Truthfully, I can't. We drove her to the hospital. They admitted her and are assessing her as we speak. But Zara was adamant that no one should visit her and that her daughter's needs should come first."

"It doesn't sound good, does it? I'll abide by her wishes. No doubt she will get in touch with us when the doctor decides to discharge her."

"I think that would be for the best. It will cause her less stress if her wishes are adhered to."

"That's frustrating for me to hear, but if you're telling me that she's all right in the main then I'm willing to believe you. I won't hold you up any longer than is necessary. We have arrangements to make and a spare bed to make up. Thank you for contacting us. Your number has come up on my phone; is it all right to call you if anything crops up with Mila? Not that I'm expecting her to be any trouble, but I think we're all aware how unpredictable teenagers can be."

"Of course. Day or night, just give me a call. And yes, teenagers can be a law unto themselves at times. Speak soon, and thank you, Mrs Walters."

"It's our pleasure. I'm sorry it had to come to this."

Sally ended the call and blew out a relieved breath. "She sounded nice with an underlying tone of wariness, I suppose you'd call it."

"She's agreed to care for Mila, at least that's a relief. I wasn't too sure how it was going to go with her, considering they haven't spoken for a some time."

"Right, now that appears to be sorted, let's see what we

can find out about Christian Starr and why he ended up on the missing list."

"I think we have a general idea why he took off, but it'll be interesting to see for ourselves if Zara was treated correctly by the officer in charge back in the day."

"Yep, I'm dying to find out."

# CHAPTER 3

Back at the station, with the relevant file in hand, Sally picked up a coffee and headed into the office, where she scan-read the documents for the next ten minutes, making copious notes about what she wanted to revisit during the course of the investigation.

*Damn, I'd better run it past DCI Green first. He always wants to know the ins and outs of a duck's arse. He'll throw a wobbly if I take the case on and keep him out of the loop.*

She took the file out to Lorne for her to go over and make the necessary notes so they could compare. "See what you make of it. I'm going to run this past the DCI. There's every chance he might tell us to ignore it and move on. However, I've read enough in that file to know that the Force gravely let Zara and her daughter down during the initial investigation."

"Really?" Lorne said. "Well, if you think that, then yes, we should give it another go. After all the other cases we've been over lately, the ones that Falkirk cocked up, it would be foolish to treat this case any differently, wouldn't it?"

"I agree. Let's hope Green agrees with that notion after I've argued the case for Zara."

"He will. You've got this."

"I hope so. Time to turn on the charm, eh?"

They all laughed.

Sally left the team to get on with their tasks and began the long journey up the winding corridor to DCI Green's office. "Hi, Lyn, any chance he can slot me in this morning for a quick one?"

She cringed as the words left her mouth, and a grin appeared on the secretary's face.

"I take it that was a bad choice of words," she teased.

Sally nodded. "Yes, not a part of my day I will be relaying to my husband this evening over dinner, that's for sure."

"I bet. Let me see what I can do for you, Sally. Do you want to take a seat?"

"No, I'm fine. I spend far too much time on my backside as it is."

Lyn smiled and left her seat. She knocked on the door to her right and entered when Green beckoned her into his inner sanctum.

Lyn reappeared a few seconds later. "He can spare you five minutes now as he has a Zoom meeting to attend with the Super or, if you think you'll need longer, he's asked if you would come back this afternoon, at around two."

Thinking the chief being in a rush to meet with her might go in her favour, Sally walked towards the door. "Now, would be great. Thanks, Lyn."

The secretary pushed open the door and whispered, "Good luck with your quick one."

Sally stared at her, her steps faltering in the doorway, the heat rising to her cheeks. "Thanks for that, Lyn."

"You're welcome. Can I get you a drink, Inspector? Something cool perhaps? It can get a touch warm in here."

"No, I've just had a coffee, but thanks all the same."

"Ah, Sally, what can I do for you on this grey, dreary day?" DCI Green said. He gestured for her to take a seat opposite him.

"Thanks for squeezing me in, sir. I wanted to run a case past you that has come to my attention after the documentary which aired the other week."

"Sounds intriguing. Can you sum it up quickly for me? We've only got five minutes… four now."

Sally did her very best and tried to gauge his reaction throughout their conversation. "I've only had a brief glance at the case notes, and from what I can tell, I don't believe the case was investigated thoroughly enough."

"Who was the officer in charge?"

"Bobby Kirkland, do you know him?"

He narrowed his eyes and stared at the wall behind Sally for a second or two. "The name rings a bell, might be worth having a chat with him. Maybe he was relying on gut instinct and decided to give the case a swerve."

"It reeks of the cases we've just dealt with. Would it be all right with you if we worked on it for a couple of weeks? It's not like we're inundated with cases at the moment. Those words never left my mouth by the way, especially in light of the meeting you'll be holding soon."

"You're safe, the Super doesn't want to discuss budgets this time round, which is a relief, because we're working with the bare minimum of staff as it is."

"Yeah and a Cold Case Team is going to be the first to go, I take it?"

"You're not wrong. Even though you guys have proved to be invaluable since the team was set up, not everyone is likely to see it that way."

"Because of the compensation aspect to a lot of the cases."

He pointed at her and then tapped the side of his nose

with his finger. "You've got it. So, I'm going to have to ask you to leave now that I've given you my blessing."

Lyn knocked and opened the door. "The Super is online, sir."

"Annoyingly punctual should be his middle name. Good luck, Inspector. Keep me informed as the investigation progresses."

"Don't I always?" She left her seat and spotted him cock an eyebrow.

"That's debatable at times."

Sally grinned and left his office, pleased with the result. She returned to the team to share the news.

"All systems go," she announced.

"Christ, that took less time than I was expecting," Lorne replied.

"I caught him at the right time. He was waiting on a call from the Super. Always a bonus when I don't have to fight for what's right. Okay, now we've been given the *Green* light..." She laughed. "See what I did there?"

The team groaned in unison.

"We got it, and most of us chose to ignore it."

Sally gestured with her head in Lorne's direction. "She's a harsh woman to please at times. Come back, Jack, all is forgiven. Talking of which, he didn't ring back, did he? Maybe I should give him a call to see what he's up to."

Lorne raised an eyebrow. "That's guilt talking. Do that and you're going to regret it. He knows where you are if he needs you. Maybe he's learnt to stand on his own two feet at last."

"Let's hope. Right, I'm going to start marking up the whiteboard. I'm disappointed you didn't beat me to it, Lorne."

"To be fair, we hadn't been given the *Green* light, so I didn't want to waste my time. See what I did there?"

"Give me strength," Sally grumbled and made her way towards the board to fill in the details. Then she turned back to Lorne and asked, "Before we do anything else, we need to trace the officer in charge, Bobby Kirkland."

Lorne shook her head. "I've already done it. He left the Force not long after he closed down the case."

Sally frowned. "Coincidence? Not that I believe in them. Might be worth having a chat with him, if we can find him."

"I've tried. Apparently, he left the area, settled in Cornwall somewhere. Want me to try and find him?"

"Yes, I think he should be our first port of call, even if our initial contact with him takes place over the phone."

"I'll try and locate him."

"Okay. I need the rest of us to go through the background information we have on file. Who was the loan company that came after Zara for the money? I want to know whether the loan was taken out years or months before they came looking for the payoff. Or are we dealing with yet another coincidence? Christian disappears and then all of a sudden the loan company comes out of the woodwork? That kind of thing will never ring true with me, and you know how I feel about coincidences. Where does someone get eighty grand from?"

"A loan shark?" Jordan suggested.

"Likely. The next question is, what did Christian do with the money? Why did he need such a vast sum? According to Zara, they didn't live extravagantly, not that I can recall."

"I'm not so sure. Zara mentioned that they frequently went away for weekends both in the UK and abroad. Those types of breaks don't come cheap, not if they took their daughter away with them every time. They would have had to have booked two rooms, more often than not."

Sally perched on the desk behind her. "You have a point. Let's chip away, see if there was anything obvious Kirkland missed before he closed the case. I still think it all happened too abruptly. From what we've learned, as soon as the loan company came after Zara and she informed Kirkland, that's when he started backing away. How long after that occurred did he leave the Force, Lorne?"

"Within a month or so."

"Sounds like he worked his notice and then waved goodbye. Pure speculation on my part, but what if he was paid off?"

"By whom?" Lorne asked.

Sally shrugged. "The loan company, so that he would stop digging into their business. Or what about Christian himself?"

"Why?"

She threw her hands in the air. "You tell me. There's something not adding up with his disappearance, and the officer in charge of his case jacks his job in within weeks of closing it down, what else are we to think? Bearing in mind how much I loathe dealing with coincidences."

"I don't think we should jump to conclusions just yet. Why don't we see what Kirkland has to say first?" Lorne said with her cautious hat on.

"You do that, and I'll create a list of people we need to speak to in the next few days." Sally collected the file from Stuart's desk. "Have you got what you need from it?"

"Yes, boss. I'm going to concentrate on any footage that was found around the dance studio the night he left. I've got the links to all I need; they should still be registered, it's only been a short while."

Sally smiled and patted him on the shoulder. "Good man. Let me know what you find. I'm wondering if it would be worth trying to trace the students from that dance class, see if they saw anything that night. I think I spotted a couple of names on the list but not many. I can't see the Starrs putting on a class with only two or three pupils in attendance, can you?"

"Worth a shot," Joanna said. "The information might be hard to locate, though, if the business folded. Depends if Zara retained the paperwork once the business was shut down."

"Hmm... there might be a problem there. I wanted to crack on with the investigation while she was in hospital without having to visit her. She needs to at least show signs that she's improving before I start hounding her, putting her under unintentional pressure."

"I understand," Joanna replied. "I'll do some digging through social media. Their Facebook or Twitter—sorry, X—pages might still be alive and kicking."

"Good shout. I'll leave that with you then."

"Now, Jordan, what chore can I task you with? I know, let's see what background information you can dig up about Christian's family and friends. You might want to check social media again, see what shows up."

"Rightio, boss."

Sally glanced up to see Lorne motioning for her to join her. "What's up?"

"I think I've found Kirkland, it's a pretty unusual name. Do you want to give it a go or do you want me to keep looking?"

"I'll take a shot at it."

Lorne scribbled down the number and handed it to Sally. She went back into her office to make the call, anticipating she would be less likely to get distracted in there.

With a slight trepidation rippling through her, she dialled the number. Kirkland answered his mobile shortly after.

"Hello, is this Bobby Kirkland?"

"It is. Who wants to know?"

"Hi, this is Detective Inspector Sally Parker from the

Norfolk Constabulary. Do you have time for a brief chat regarding an old case of yours?"

"I can spare you five minutes. What case?"

"The Christian Starr case."

The line went dead. Sally held the phone away from her ear and checked the signal on her mobile. It was the best she'd known it, so there was no excuse for the line to get disconnected, unless there was a problem at Kirkland's end. Undeterred, she rang his number again. This time she used the landline, hoping that would be more stable. The phone rang four times before Kirkland answered again.

"Not sure what happened there," she said. "The signal was good at my end."

"I'm in Cornwall, it can be a bit dodgy down here. What do you want to know? And why? Has Starr shown up?"

"No, but his wife is a friend of a friend and has asked me to cast my eye over the case. I was surprised to learn that you had retired at such a young age. May I ask why?"

"Because my wife was seriously ill with cancer and the stress of the job was getting to both of us. We moved areas to be with her family. She was born in Falmouth and wanted to be buried down here."

"Buried? Are you telling me that she didn't pull through?"

"That's right. She had terminal bowel cancer. They did their best for her, but she died at the end of last year."

"That's so sad, I'm sorry to hear that. Are you planning to stay down there or are you going to return to Norfolk?"

"I've met someone else, a local girl, so the intention is to stay here. Sorry, I need to go out soon, I have a dentist's appointment."

"I won't keep you too long. How well can you remember the case?"

"Pretty well. Why?"

"Well, I've only taken on the case this morning and briefly

read the case notes. The thing that jumped out at me was that you didn't seem to give it a chance to get going. Can you tell me why?"

"Tell me, Inspector, how often do you work on your gut instinct?"

"Ninety percent of the time, with an added caveat, I don't think I've ever walked away from a case without having the proof to back up that instinct."

"Well, I suppose that's where we differ. As soon as I met Mrs Starr, Zara, isn't it?"

"That's correct."

"I had a feeling that things didn't add up."

"Can you explain why? Having met her today, all I saw was a very broken woman—I might add, on the verge of death. Actually, my partner and I had to drive her to the hospital where she was admitted right away."

"That's sad. I hope she isn't in there too long. I always got the impression that she was holding back on me about their relationship."

"You didn't think they were head over heels in love, living life to the full as a successful couple running a dance studio?"

"Not in the slightest, and the daughter, who would have been sixteen at the time, if my memory serves me right, she was never around for me to interview. I invited her to come down to the station to see me, through her mother, but she never took me up on my offer. Don't you find that strange?"

"Maybe. How long did you give her, around a week?"

"Yes, that's right."

"Maybe she had a hectic after-school life that she struggled to juggle in order to pay you a visit. Did you ever put yourself out and call back to the house to see her after your shift had ended?"

"No, because my wife's condition stood in the way. Perhaps I'm guilty of not giving the case my undivided attention, however, in my defence it was extremely hard to ditch the gut feeling I was having about Zara, and then when she contacted me about the debts that had come to light, that was the last straw for me. It was obvious the husband had got cold feet and done a runner."

"I see. Hmm... I'm not sure how I would have reacted if things went down as you've described them. Did you find any leads to go on regarding Christian's disappearance?"

"Not really. What I did find was all noted in the file. I'm sorry, I've got to go now."

"Okay, I'll have a thorough check through your notes. Would it be okay to contact you if I have any queries in the future?"

"Of course. I have nothing to hide, Inspector. I sensed when we first spoke that you were treating me as a suspect."

"I apologise if it came across that way. It was the fact you left the Force not long after you had closed the case down that drew my attention. Thanks for speaking to me today."

"You're welcome. I guess it would be wrong of me not to offer you any advice for the future. Nevertheless, I would be careful of Mrs Starr. I got the impression that she was trying to dupe me every time I spoke with her."

"I'll take that advice on board. Take care, and thanks for taking my call today. Good luck at the dentist."

"I'm going to need it. I have a hefty bill to pay after a lengthy stay in his chair for treatment today."

"Ouch! I hope it's not too painful in both respects." Sally ended the call and sat back to consider what he'd told her. She hadn't anticipated the conversation going in that direction at all so found herself confused. She picked up the file and instead of scan-reading it, this time she read the notes word for word, or more or less. She concentrated on what type of investigations Kirkland had carried out surrounding the husband's disappearance, only to find it was minimal at best. A few searches on the CCTV footage, but he hadn't used the ANPR cameras around the area to track Christian's vehicle at all, which struck Sally as odd.

There was a knock at the door. "Come in."

Lorne opened the door and held up a mug of coffee. "I thought you might be needing another one by now."

Sally sat forward and peered into the mug on her desk. She tutted. "Yep, I only managed to drink half of the last one. How are things going out there?"

"I'd say some interesting things are coming to light from everyone. How did you get on with Kirkland?"

"Sounds intriguing. I know I've said this a lot lately, but having spoken to him, I find myself getting splinters in my backside."

Lorne placed the mug on the desk and sat. "Did he willingly cooperate?"

"He did, after a while. I rang him on my mobile, introduced myself, and the phone immediately went dead which put my hackles up. Undeterred, I rang him back on the landline and found he opened up to me easily... perhaps too easily." She chewed on her lip, wondering if she was doing him an injustice.

"What sort of things did he say that could put you in a quandary?"

Sally relayed the conversation and watched Lorne's reaction throughout her summation. "What do you think?"

"He seemed to go on about working on his gut instinct a lot and yet he walked away from the investigation."

"That's what I pointed out to him when he asked how I dealt with a gut instinct. As a copper, you do anything and everything to prove your feelings about a case or a person involved are right, don't you? How many times have you thrown your hands up in the air and walked away from an ongoing case?"

"Exactly, especially after the money issue came to light. Wouldn't you explore that side of things before you put an investigation to bed?"

"I would, and I know you would, too. Any news on that side of things? Hang on, before you answer that, what do you think about the story he told about his wife? That should be easy to verify, shouldn't it?"

"I can do that for you now, if you want?"

"Yes, if you would. What about the loans?"

"As far as we can tell they were from loan sharks. Maybe they heard about the case through the media and decided to get their money back quickly from Zara before she collapsed into a heap and let the bank take the house from her. I don't know if that's the case, but it seems a likely scenario to me, having dealt with a few of these despots in the past."

Sally smiled. "Not personally, I hope?"

"Christ, no. Let me do some digging about his wife. To me, it sounds like you have the right to feel cautious about him. You know what men are like when dealing with an emotional woman. Most of them have a severe problem handling the issue."

"I agree. I think I'm going to set aside the conversation I had with him and stick to the facts as I see them. Look at the state Zara was in earlier. If the woman knew something or was hiding anything to do with her husband's disappearance, would she have truly cut herself off from her family or even got rid of the house they were living in, to take on the property, or should I say dump, she's sharing with her daughter now? It doesn't ring true, does it?"

"No, I'd be inclined to agree with you. I know it's early days yet, but dealing with the facts is definitely the way to go, Sal. The poor woman was hanging on to a bloody thread when we knocked on her door this morning."

"Heartbreaking to see her that way. If she had anything to

hide, as Kirkland seems to think she had, then she wouldn't have got into such a state, surely."

"Yep, go with your own gut instinct and ignore what he said, that would be my advice. We can revisit it if any doubts creep in later as the investigation progresses, of course. What's our next step?"

"I want to see what the team comes back with first and then start interviewing the rest of the family, see what they can tell us. Looking at the file, I don't think Kirkland questioned many of them, if any."

"What did he do then? Nothing, or so it would seem. Even more reason to take what he says with a pinch of salt. I'll check what happened to his wife."

"Let me know the second you find out. If he's lying, then I'm afraid we're going to have to put him down as a person of interest, as much as that grieves me to say about one of our own."

"Needs must in some cases. Look how bent Falkirk turned out to be."

"You don't have to remind me. That man's name will continue to be the bane of my life until the day I die."

"Don't let the fucker eat away at you, he's not worth it. Over the last couple of years, you and the team have worked wonders righting his wrongs in the community."

"I know, but that con artist, depraved individual, shouldn't have been allowed to get away with what he did to all those people. The unfortunate ones who died in prison, who went on to be found innocent. Is it any wonder the general public's perception of the police in this country is at an all-time low?"

"Hey, we can take comfort in the fact that neither one of us has ever been on the receiving end of any bad publicity for the work we've covered over the years. The same can't be said for our male counterparts, so keep that uppermost in your mind, and we'll continue to have a blast. Policing and serving our community are in our blood. Christ, they have to be, the number of times I've revoked my retirement over the years."

"Yeah, you've either got a screw loose or you're one hell of a committed woman, Lorne Warner."

"Are you saying I should be committed?"

They both laughed.

"Who knows? The stuff we have to endure daily with this career."

"We could debate this topic for days, but it's not going to help us solve this case, if there's a case to solve."

"You're right. All it's doing is making us more and more depressed. Let's get back to it. I'll finish going over the file and join you soon."

WITH NOTHING else of interest catching her eye, Sally put the file to one side and left her office. "Right, what news do you have for me?"

Joanna raised her hand first. Sally crossed the room and drew out a chair at the desk next to hers.

"I searched through the social media accounts and found certain posts from the dance studio announcing the latest classes, although none of them mentioned how many slots were available."

"So, we have no way of knowing who the students were who attended that night? That's a shame. Maybe there was some kind of disturbance at the club, either between some of the students and Christian jumped in to break it up, or more likely that Christian himself was involved."

Joanna shrugged. "There's just no way of knowing, not unless someone comes forward during the investigation. Will you be putting out a plea for the public's help soon?"

Sally sighed and puffed out her cheeks, her indecision whirling in her head. "I think we need to find something substantial before we even consider doing one. Maybe you've just found it. Let's hang fire on making that decision for now. Thanks, Joanna. Keep searching, see if you can find any form of disruption or anger attached to the dance studio's posts over the years, if you will?"

"Sure. I'll let you know."

Sally stood and tucked her chair back under the desk again and moved around the room to Stuart. "Any luck with chasing up the links on the CCTV footage?"

"I did, but there really wasn't much to see. He left the dance studio; there was a disc on file from the building itself. No one approached him in the car park as he walked to his vehicle, absolutely zilch. He drove away. The car didn't have any visible faults with it. There was more footage further down that long stretch of road, which caught his car and, again, no sign of him being followed or anything else out of the ordinary. And that was the last anyone saw of him and his vehicle that night. For some reason, the officer in charge…" He checked his notepad for the name. "Kirkland, didn't request any ANPR footage. That's the part that I'm finding incredibly hard to believe."

"I said the same myself to Lorne in the office not half an hour ago. It beggars belief. The jury is still out for me on that. We know how important the first twenty-four hours are in any investigation, but not everyone thinks like us, especially when the person has been reported missing." Sally held her arms out to the sides and let them fall again. "I give up with some of our colleagues and their attitudes to work. Yes, maybe we can make an exception for Kirkland if his attention lay elsewhere, with his wife undergoing treatment for cancer, but Christ, we've all been through the wringer whilst on duty at one time or another, haven't we?"

"We certainly have," Lorne chipped in.

"Yep, you're at the head of the queue, Lorne, with what you had to overcome when Charlie was abducted by that... fiend, shall we call him?"

"Yeah, amongst other things. Sorry to interrupt your conversation, I have some news for you."

"About his wife?"

Lorne nodded. "It's as expected, he was telling the truth. She passed away at the end of twenty-two from bowel cancer. That's what is stated on her death certificate, so it must be true."

"Hmm... okay, again, if that's the case, I think I'm prepared to give him the benefit of the doubt for ballsing up this investigation. So, unless Jordan has discovered anything bad about the family via their social media accounts... Have you?"

"Nothing notable as yet, boss, but I've only trawled back to around the time Christian went missing. Want me to go back further?"

"Yes, go back at least five years. Also, can you give me a list of the names Zara interacted with the most? We'll need to try and find her friends. I want to cover all the angles swiftly and interview friends and family to get an overview of the possible circumstances behind his disappearance. Whether the marriage was on an upward swing or a downhill slide, and I'm going to need you guys to help with the interviews so we can cover all the bases over the next few days."

"Just Zara's friends, or shall I make a list of Christian's, too?"

Sally winked at him. "Yes, both. Thanks, Jordan."

"It shouldn't take too long; he was less active on social media than his wife. Funny, that." He smiled.

"What are you trying to say? Or would you like to retract that statement?" She grinned.

Jordan's cheeks coloured up. "I think I've said enough already. I'd better get back to work now, boss."

"While you do that, I'm going to ring the hospital check how Zara is and then, when I come back, will make a plan of action of what we do next," she announced over her shoulder as she walked back to her office.

Once inside, she heaved out a relieved sigh. At last she had the feeling that they were doing the right thing by revisiting the case, although she had no idea what the outcome was likely to be.

*Are you still alive, Christian? Did someone kidnap you that night and kill you?*

She still had major reservations about the last scenario, the main reason being because of the debts and the deception leading up to that devastating revelation. She tried to put herself in Zara's shoes, but that steered her mind in a direction she no longer wished to revisit: her first marriage to the dreaded Darryl.

She bashed the sides of her head with her hands and whispered, "Get out, you have no right being in there, none whatsoever. I'm over you and I have been for years."

"You tell him."

Sally spun around to find Lorne standing there. "Sorry... it's just that..."

Lorne reached out her arms, and Sally walked into them.

"You never have to apologise to me. We both have certain demons lurking that come to the surface now and again. This time round it's your turn, a few months ago, it was mine. That makes us even in my book."

Sally pulled back and smiled. "Memories, evil ones at that. Is that God's way of punishing us now and again, to keep us in line?"

Lorne sighed and shrugged. "Maybe, who knows?"

"I'm fine, don't worry about me. I'll see if there's any news about Zara, and then we'll get on the road again. How does that sound to you?"

"Like you're back in the game and know exactly how to progress with the case, so stop doubting yourself."

"Thanks, pal. I'm so glad to have an understanding partner by my side for a change. Jack had a habit of fobbing my feelings off at times. Mostly telling me to keep my time of the month under control. He didn't come out with those words exactly, but the inference was always there nevertheless."

"Typical of Jack. Have you still not heard from him?"

"Nope. I'll leave it a couple of days and check in with him if the situation is still the same. I know I'm a worrywart."

"No, you're a caring and loyal friend to so many. I'll leave you to it."

"Thanks again, Lorne. I shouldn't be too long."

Lorne eased out of the office, and Sally made her way to her desk. She was fortunate to ring the ward where they had left Zara at just the right time, because the doctor she had spoken to, who had attended to Zara, happened to be standing at the nurses' station and willingly gave her an update on the poor woman.

"Ah, yes, Inspector. I've not long checked on Zara. She seems much more positive than when she was first admitted. The psychiatrist is in there with her now, that's why I'm hanging around, so we can compare notes. My honest opinion is that we won't need to section her. But it's going to be her responsibility to handle her life better. You saw how vulnerable she was. She's already told me that she is estranged from her family. Maybe you can do something to address that by reaching out to them? It's just a suggestion, I'm not for one second trying to tell you how to do your job."

"Already initiated, Doctor. Her daughter will be staying

with Zara's parents for the time being. I was just checking in on Zara before I head over there to see them."

"Good. Family are very important resources, who sadly many choose to ignore at times, until something like this comes their way. I don't mind admitting that I was horrified to see her in such a state when you brought her in. I fear that another couple of days of not caring for herself properly and she would no longer be with us."

"We have her friend to thank for Zara coming to our attention. If she hadn't contacted me today then... still, that side of things isn't worth worrying about now, is it?"

"Don't get me wrong, she's far from out of the woods yet, but there are glimpses of her improving, even at this early stage."

"That's reassuring to hear. I should have left you my card. Can you jot down my number and contact me directly if things take a turn for the worse?"

"Of course. I have a pen ready."

Sally gave the doctor her mobile number. "Ring me day or night. I really care about what happens to her. The woman has been through a living nightmare the last couple of years. Her world has been turned upside down."

"I know. I take my hat off to you for trying to assist her. Maybe knowing that someone is finally listening to her concerns will be the push she needs to get her life back on track once more. Maybe she'll be able to mend the broken bridges that exist between her and her family members."

"I'll need to keep my fingers crossed on that one. Thanks for speaking with me, Doctor, I realise how busy your days must be, and thank you for taking special care of Zara."

"There's really no need. I'm only doing my job, as you are. However, there are certain people's plights that pull at our heartstrings, I'm sure you'll agree, Inspector."

"Absolutely. Take care."

"You, too."

Sally ended the call feeling far more positive about Zara's future well-being than she had been when they'd last seen her.

*Onwards and upwards, Zara. You might not think it, but you have so much in this life to live for, and we're going to do our best to find out what happened to Christian and maybe get you all back together as a family again, soon.*

# CHAPTER 4

In the car, Sally slapped a hand over her mouth, covering the yawn that came out of nowhere. "It's been a long day, and we're not even halfway through it yet."

"It has been emotionally draining for you. You've been running on adrenaline for hours and, apart from the sugar rush we obtained from the cakes we munched on this morning, we haven't found the time to stop for lunch."

"Hark at you. Is that a dig?"

"Not in the slightest."

"We'll see how things go with the grandparents and then possibly rectify that afterwards, how does that sound?"

Lorne rubbed her stomach. "Good to me. This is a much nicer area, isn't it? I wonder why her parents didn't open their home up to Zara and Mila."

"I suppose we'll get the lowdown on that during our conversation with them. Are you ready for this? It's too early for Mila to be home from school yet, so we should be able to get the parents to speak freely without them thinking Mila is going to walk in on us."

"Here's hoping."

A woman was standing at the window at the front of the house, waiting for them to arrive after Lorne had rung ahead, telling Zara's parents to expect them. She left her position when Sally pushed open the gate. She removed her ID from her pocket and flashed it once Mrs Walters opened the door. There was no smile to greet them, just an anxious nibble of the lip.

"Hello, we've been expecting you. Let me call my husband, he's out in the garden, tidying up out there, what with spring being just around the corner, according to him anyway. It's still the dead of winter for me. Come in, ladies. Can I get you a drink?"

"Two coffees, white with one sugar, if you don't mind," Sally said.

"First door on the right, make yourselves at home."

They entered the lounge and took a seat on the sofa. The room was larger than Sally had anticipated. She suspected it had been two rooms and knocked into one sometime in the not-too-distant past, judging by the way it had been decorated and how new the furniture looked.

There was a feature fireplace in the chimney breast with a small wood-burning stove and an oak mantel above. The cushions on the grey-covered sofas complimented some of the mustard colour in the curtains.

"Takes me back to when I used to renovate houses," Lorne said.

"Hey, you've still got the knack. Those mood boards you created for Tony and Simon to use on the last couple of houses they've put back on the market proves that point."

"This is so warm and welcoming. Whoever created this has a real flair for interior design. I wonder if the wife did it or if they enlisted the help of a professional."

"We could ask. You're really smitten with it, aren't you?"

"And some."

The door opened, and Mrs Walters came in carrying a tray with mugs and a plate of biscuits, which she set on the coffee table in front of Sally and Lorne. She opened the drawer underneath and removed a couple of wooden coasters which she set out for each of them. Behind her, a man followed her into the room and made his way over to the armchair beside Sally.

"This is my husband, Leslie, and I'm Amy. I'm sorry, I didn't really catch your names at the door."

"I'm Sally, and this is Lorne. Thanks so much for agreeing to see us today and for reaching out to take care of Mila. Did you manage to contact the school?"

"Yes, they've asked her to visit the headmaster before she leaves the grounds. Leslie is going to go down there to pick her up at three-thirty, aren't you, dear?"

"It's the least I can do after what that young lady has been through by the sounds of it. Have you heard how our daughter is doing?" He picked up a mug from the tray and cradled it in his hands, probably warming them after working in the garden on a chilly day.

"Yes, I checked in with them and managed to speak to the doctor who admitted Zara. She was being assessed by the psychiatrist. She reassured me that she didn't think Zara would need to be sectioned as first suspected."

"Sectioned? Under the Mental Health Act?" Amy asked, shocked. She removed a mug and a shortbread biscuit and sat on the arm of her husband's chair. "I didn't think she would be that bad. What diagnosis has this doctor given you?"

Sally inhaled a large breath and let it seep out slowly while she chose her words carefully. "I really didn't want to tell you this over the phone, but when we showed up at your daughter's home this morning... let's just say she was very poorly indeed."

"But you said she was suffering from exhaustion; did you lie to me?"

"Maybe I side-stepped the truth a little, only because I didn't want you to worry. This sort of news should be shared face to face, not over the telephone. That's the way I prefer to work, anyway."

"Fair enough. Can you be honest with us now and tell us how bad she really is?"

"I really don't want to worry you further, and Zara has insisted that you shouldn't go and see her yet, not until she's on the road to recovery."

Amy put her mug on a coaster and reached for a tissue as the tears began to fall. She retook her seat, and her husband hooked an arm around her waist.

"We've let her down, haven't we?" Amy sobbed.

"Now stop that, it was her decision not to see us, not ours. We showed that girl nothing but kindness and support, and she slammed the door in our faces," Leslie replied.

"Funny how we always see things like this differently."

"It shouldn't matter what has taken place in the past," Sally interrupted, sensing an argument brewing between the husband and wife. "I get the sense that Zara has been suffering badly not having her family around her over the last couple of years." She continued, not holding back, her concern for Zara evident. "Perhaps you can tell me the circumstances behind the falling-out you've had with your daughter?"

"Isn't it obvious?" Leslie bit back.

"Not to an outsider, sorry. Your daughter's husband went missing, and she was struggling to cope when the debts began rolling in."

They both bowed their heads in shame, and it was Amy who eventually replied.

"Our daughter refused to listen to our advice, and that's

when things became heated. Her head was all over the place. She was confused, and her decision-making proved to be questionable. We did our best for her, neither of us wanted to see her move into the house she's in now. She had a beautiful home, but it turned out to be mortgaged to the hilt. So, she had that to contend with as well as the other debts that came in. Fortunately, we had money tied up in a trust fund for her that she could get her hands on. It was an inheritance from her grandparents; they insisted it should go into a trust and not be touched unless there was a dire need to use it."

"I don't understand. If you had money set aside for her, why on earth did you fall out?"

"Because we've always kept it a secret from the three children. We waited until the last minute to tell her. She's never forgiven us for that. Even though it wouldn't have been enough to get her out of the hole she was in. That's when our relationship went to pot, sank to an all-time low. We loved our daughter, still do, but all we're guilty of doing is protecting her. We thought we were doing the right thing at the time, never expected it to backfire in the way it did. We regret not stepping in sooner, I can assure you."

"Did you try and tell her that?"

"Of course we did. By that time, it was too late and she refused to speak to us. Their absence in our lives has left a huge hole in our hearts. We're so glad to have this opportunity to start afresh, if she'll allow us to. I'm glad she's reached out, if only through you, for us to care for our granddaughter. It means so much to us."

"Time for you to rebuild the bridges."

"We truly want that, don't we, Leslie?" Amy smiled at her husband.

"More than anything in this world. We've missed our daughter, we all have, even Perry and Julie have mentioned it lately, how much they've missed their sister and Mila. We were such a close unit until the day he went missing. Are you reopening the case?"

"We're considering it. Kim, Zara's good friend, is a friend of mine, and she's pleaded with me to at least take another look at the case. My team and I have spent most of the day doing just that. The next step was to come and see you, to get your take on what happened around the time."

The couple glanced at each other.

"What can we say?" Leslie asked. "We did everything we could to try and find the lad. The next day, Perry and I drove around the area for three or four hours but found nothing, no sign of his car, nothing."

"What do you believe happened?" Sally asked.

He shook his head. "In the beginning, I believed that something sinister had gone on."

"And when did that belief change?" Sally demanded.

"A few days afterwards. With no sign of him or his car, and when the first loan demand came through the door, we realised there was more to this than we first thought. But Zara wouldn't see it. She was determined to cling on to the idea that something serious had happened to Christian. It turned out to be an awkward situation, us thinking one thing and her believing another, and yet neither of us was prepared to see the other's point of view, or worse still, back down and consider what the other was saying."

"And that's when things escalated and the divide between you widened?"

"That's right," Amy agreed. "It was extremely hard for me; I was stuck in the middle. Yes, Leslie thought he was speaking for me, for us as a couple, but I had major doubts lingering in my mind that I kept to myself. I let her down and, for that knowing where all this has ended, I will always feel a deep sense of guilt."

"I never knew you felt that way, Amy. Why would you

keep something as important as that from me?" Leslie asked before Sally could respond.

Amy leapt to her feet and glared at him. "Because you've never let me have a say over the years, not where the kids and their upbringing were concerned." She paced the floor and added, "Why didn't I put my foot down?"

"I can't believe you're saying all of this after keeping quiet about it for so long." Leslie raked a hand through his hair.

"It was my aim to have a peaceful life, but at what cost? What it boils down to is that our daughter needed us, and we essentially kicked her into touch because she didn't agree with your point of view. What kind of people does that make us look like? A woman and her child are out there, desperate, and *we* turned our backs on them," Amy screeched, the colour rising up her neck.

Feeling the need to step in, if only to calm things down a little, Sally said, "Please, there's no need for you to go over what's gone on in the past, not in this instance, not when there's a chance for you to put things right. Your names cropped up immediately with Zara as people she could rely on to care for her daughter, your granddaughter. In my opinion, that speaks volumes about your relationship and possibly how much she wants to heal the rift that is lingering between you."

Amy retook her seat, and her husband gathered her hand in his.

"The inspector is right. Maybe she's giving us the chance to start again. I'm willing to forgive and forget, if she is."

Amy kissed him on the cheek. "Thank you. I think you're doing the right thing, for all of us. Can you imagine how uncomfortable Mila is going to feel if she overhears us bickering all the time, slagging off her mother?"

"I would never do that," he stated adamantly.

Amy cocked an eyebrow. "Another thing we appear to

differ on." She smiled. "We've been given a second chance to make amends, we need to swallow our pride and be there for Zara."

"I agree."

Sally and Lorne smiled at each other.

"That's going to make things so much better, for all of you," Sally said. "In situations like this, a lot of people would have stubbornly stood their ground. Not been prepared to recognise their daughter's pleas for help. Believe me, she really needs it."

"You keep intimating that she's really sick, and yet we're not allowed to visit her," Amy said. "Why? If she's reached out and asked us to care for Mila when she's in hospital, why on earth won't she allow us to go and see her?"

"She has her reasons," Leslie replied. "Rather than let our minds race ahead, why don't we be satisfied with what she's given us, for now?"

Amy nodded. "Okay." She faced Sally and said, "But if our daughter deteriorates, will you tell us?"

"Don't worry, I will."

"So, what happens now?" Leslie asked. "Regarding the investigation?"

"We're going to need to reinterview everyone highlighted in the original file, just to make sure the officer in charge didn't miss anything important."

"And if he did? Two years later, what will you be able to do about it?"

"It depends on what comes to light. We'll follow up any new leads and go from there. In my experience—sorry, our experience—the slightest of clues can go a long way towards solving a case. I find having a positive attitude always helps, too."

"You're going to need it," Leslie said with a glimmer of a smile, his previous anger long dispersed.

"Is there anything else you feel we should look into?"

The couple stared at each other, their brows knitted, and they both shook their heads.

"No, not that we can think of," Amy replied. She glanced up at the clock on the wall. "Leslie, it's nearly time for you to head off to the school. Don't forget Mila will need to go home to pack an overnight bag, at least."

He nodded and stood. "It was nice meeting you both. I want to assure you that we're going to do everything we can to make our daughter better again, and we, or should I say I, will ensure I never let either of them down in the future."

"That's music to my ears, Mr Walters. A word of caution, don't expect too much too soon, from either Zara or Mila. Just stand back a little and see where the land lies once Mila has stayed with you for a few days. I'm sure knowing that she's safe will have a significant impact on Zara's recovery."

"Let's hope so." He kissed Amy on the cheek and left the room.

Amy stared out of the front window, watched him get in the car and whispered, "His heart has always been in the right place, but he's stubborn to the core."

"The turnaround in him was remarkable," Sally said, "so maybe there's a genuine desire to right the wrongs of the past. It's not something we've witnessed that often, a three-sixty-degree turn like that, so I have high hopes for him."

"Thank you, that's a relief to hear. You must deal with a lot of emotional outbursts in similar circumstances."

"We do. We have to judge each one on its merits. I have a good feeling that your reunion with Zara, when it happens, will be a good one."

"I hope so. We have a lot of making up to do, not only with her but with Mila as well. Basically, we were in the wrong, and it's up to us to show them nothing but love and support from now on."

"That's definitely the way to go. Do you think it would be possible to speak with your other children, Julie and Perry, today? I'm presuming they'll be at work at this time of day."

"Yes, they both work. Julie is a primary school teacher, so she'll be home at around four, maybe a little after, and Perry, he's an IT consultant. Most days he works from home."

"Great, can we trouble you for their addresses? It would be better if we saw them soon. That way we can get the ball rolling on the investigation early."

"Let me get my phone, it'll be in my contacts. I'm no good with house numbers. I could drive you there, but…"

Sally smiled. "I'm the same."

Amy collected her mobile from the side table next to Lorne and opened it. Lorne withdrew her notebook and jotted down the details.

"Brilliant, thank you," Lorne replied.

"I hope they'll be able to remember what we couldn't, but I doubt it."

"It's worth a shot. Are you going to be all right by yourself?" Sally asked.

"Yes, yes, don't worry about me. I'll go upstairs and have a root around, see what little welcoming knick-knacks I can put in Mila's room. I'm so excited to see her, it's been far too long not to have them in my life."

"These things happen. Try not to dwell on it or let it come between you and your husband."

"That's good advice. I'll take that on board, thank you. I'll show you out, ladies."

At the front door, Sally extended her hand. "Take care and keep that beautiful smile on your face."

Amy squeezed her hand tighter. "Thank you. This is going to be such a wonderful experience, having Mila here with us. I don't think I will ever stop smiling again."

"Good. Speak soon."

They left the house and, once Sally reached the car, she glanced back to see Amy standing in the window of the lounge, this time happiness radiating from her instead of anxiety.

Back in the car, Lorne said, "She's a lovely lady. The situation between them must have driven her to the edge and back."

"Possibly. I have an inkling that it has affected Zara far more over the years, though."

"Sorry, yes, I didn't mean that to sound so blasé."

"You didn't, maybe I was simply pointing out the obvious. Onwards. We'll try Perry first."

Lorne took the hint and added the postcode to the satnav. His property turned out to be five minutes away from his parents'. It was an apartment in a small newly built block that Sally remembered being constructed around five years before.

"I always thought these places had a good feel about them. What a great location, overlooking the town and not that far from the river."

"They're not too high either, not what I regard as a blot on the landscape. Instead, they appear to enhance the surroundings. Or is that a silly observation?"

Sally laughed. "No, I would call it a Lorne observation and, you're right. I couldn't have put it better myself. Come on, we can't hang around out here all day, the wind is getting up again."

They hadn't tried to ring ahead, like they had with his parents, so they had no idea what type of reception they were going to get.

Perry Walters opened the door sporting a frown. He looked them up and down. "Can I help?"

"Perry Walters?" Sally asked. She produced her warrant card. "I'm DI Sally Parker, and this is my partner, DS Lorne

Warner. Would it be possible to come in and have a brief chat with you?"

"I'm Perry. The police, you say? What's this about?"

"Inside would be better, unless it's not convenient?" Sally queried.

"Is it ever convenient, to sit down and have a conversation with the police?" His retort was short and snappy. Nevertheless, after a second or two he took a step back and gestured for them to enter.

"Thanks. We won't keep you long, I promise."

"You still haven't told me what this is all about. Come into the lounge."

They followed him up the narrow hallway to an open-plan lounge-cum-kitchen at the rear. The view was outstanding, taking in the river and the fields beyond.

"This is a lovely apartment, did you buy it from new?" Sally asked.

"I did. I put my name down before the foundations were set in the ground. I love it here. Take a seat. I'll just shut down my computer. I work from home most days but have to show my face at the office once a week."

"Do you prefer to work that way, in isolation?" Sally asked.

She and Lorne sat on the stylish two-seater couch with its metal arms and legs while Perry pulled a leather beanbag across from the other side of the room. "Yep, suits me."

"First of all, I want to thank you for seeing us without an appointment. We've just come from your parents' house."

He dug his elbows into his knees and leaned forward. "Are they all right? I haven't spoken to them for a week or so."

"Yes, they're fine. Let me run through what's happened today, to give you a better idea of why we're here."

"Please do. Sorry, I should have asked, do you want a drink? Am I going to need one?"

"We're fine. But help yourself, if you need one."

"I was teasing. I meant an alcoholic one for any shock I'm about to receive."

"No shock value, I promise." Sally recapped the meeting they'd held first thing with Kim and what that had led to.

He listened intently and appeared to be interested until Sally mentioned that they had taken Zara to hospital.

"I can believe it… she's always preferred to be the centre of attention, that one."

"You don't get along?"

"Occasionally. When it's not all about her."

"Is she an attention-seeker? Is that what you're telling us?"

"You need to make up your own mind about that. Speaking from experience, I grew up in the same house with two sisters, and they couldn't have been more different. We knew Zara would turn out to be in the entertainment industry, in one way or another. I suppose she saw starting up the dance studio with Christian as maybe a start on the road to that. Everything centred around her, and Julie and I never really got a look-in with our parents. Julie will back me up if you're intending to interview her as well."

"Were you resentful of that fact?"

"No, well, I suppose, in my younger days. I got into a bit of mischief at school. It was the only attention I ever got from my parents."

"Sorry to hear that you had to go to such extremes."

"I'm over it. My parents and I get along okay today, that's all that counts. I think with Zara being off the scene for a while it's been good for Julie and me to rebuild our non-existent relationship with our parents. If that makes sense?"

"It does. Your parents seemed distraught about Zara being admitted to hospital."

"They would be. I don't know what more I can say. If you want to show someone the definition of what a dysfunctional family looks like, then please, send them our way."

Sally smiled and wondered if what Perry was telling them should put him on the suspect list. "What about Christian, did you get on with him?"

"In small doses. He was a bit up his own arse at times, too. Some might say they made an ideal couple. But I still stepped up and helped Dad search for him, the night he went missing and for the next few days. We hunted high and low for that man, for what? Nothing, it was a complete time-suck for us."

"Time-suck? Because of your lack of success?"

"That and because of what happened next that ended up putting huge doubts in my mind."

Sally inclined her head.

"Don't tell me you're not aware of the debts he accrued, against the house and the business?" he said. "At least that's what we were told."

"Why say that? Didn't you see the proof?"

"Oh yes, I meant, knowing my sister and how much she liked to spend, I wouldn't have put it past her to have put her signature to the loans and blame her hubby, once he went missing, you know, to make him look bad and her ending up smelling like roses."

"Ouch, that's a bit harsh, isn't it?"

He stared at the floor between them and shrugged. "You'd say the same if you knew my sister the way I do."

"May I ask what you suspect happened to Christian?"

"I've always had a hunch that he'd had enough and just took off somewhere."

"Was there any indication of him being unsettled leading up to his disappearance?"

He paused to think before he spoke again. "It's been a while since I've really thought about it. Had you asked me that question back in the day, I would have probably been able to answer it without any hesitation, now I'm not so sure."

"Take your time, we're in no rush. If you can consider anything that could possibly have occurred in the months leading up to him going missing?"

"No, that won't work, as I've already told you, we weren't that close. I only volunteered my services to search for him to appease my parents, out of necessity, not because I really wanted to do it out of respect for either Zara or Christian."

"I see. There really was an immense rift between you, wasn't there?"

"Yes. When you've lived under a cloud all your life, it's very hard to shift it."

"I'm sorry you feel that way. Has your relationship with your parents improved since Zara has been out of the picture?"

"Considerably, but I suppose you'd say it was with an underlying reluctance."

"I think I understand what you mean. You weren't kidding when you said your family was dysfunctional." Sally smiled.

His only response was to shrug again. "I don't know what else to tell you."

"This might sound a bit of a silly question as I'm sure you would have already mentioned it if it had happened… have you ever heard from or seen Christian since?"

"Never, not even a case of mistaken identity, you know, a possible fleeting glance when I've been on a night out in town."

"If you believe he's still alive, do you think he's moved far away from Norfolk?"

"Your guess is as good as mine. I don't know how you're

going to find out. Would that sort of thing show up on your system?"

"Sadly, not if he's changed his identity. We'd need to have a name to check first. Can you tell us if he had any good friends he hung around with?"

"I can't because I wasn't close to him. I never joined any WhatsApp chats they set up with the family or even friended him on Facebook, why would I?"

"Fair enough. Okay, I think we're done here. I'll give you a card. If you think of anything that you feel might be of interest to the investigation, will you give me a call?"

"I'll do that."

They all stood. Sally handed him a card at the front door.

"I hope you find him, if he's still alive, just don't bring him anywhere near me, not after the disruption and pain he has caused every member of my family. The man is the lowest of the low if he's still alive and saw fit to walk away, rather than face his responsibilities."

"Well, we'll have to see about that, won't we? Thank you for sparing us the time today."

"You're welcome. Sorry if I came across as unsympathetic to what's going on with my sister. I suppose you would have needed to have lived in my shoes for a few decades to totally understand what's going on up here and in here." He tapped his temple and then held a clenched fist over his heart.

At a loss what to say next, Sally smiled and nodded. "Enjoy your evening."

"What did you make of that?" Lorne asked on the way back to the vehicle.

Sally sighed heavily. "I really don't know. At first, I considered putting him at the top of the suspect list, now, I'm not so sure. I guess all it's proving so far is just how blind we are, going into this investigation."

"Yeah, that thought crossed my mind several times

throughout that conversation. Do you think it's true, what he said about Zara putting her signature on the loan forms?"

"It's hard to tell, isn't it? He's visibly still angry about what he's had to contend with during his life. How do we know it's not sour grapes getting in the way? Again, I think the only way we're going to get anywhere with this case is if we stick to the facts."

"I agree, not that there are many to hand at present. I wonder what the sister is going to tell us."

"There's only one way we're going to find out. Let's go and see her, then call it a day."

# CHAPTER 5

When they drove to Julie's house, a small brick-built terrace, they found it empty. As it was only four-fifteen and Amy Walters had told them her daughter usually got home at around four, they took the decision to sit in the car and wait for her.

"This is a possibility," Lorne said.

Sally peered into her rear-view mirror and saw a woman in her mid-thirties getting out of a car a couple of spaces behind them. She went to her boot, unloaded three carrier bags and walked past them towards the house.

"I think you're right."

They got out and approached the woman.

"Julie Granger?" Sally asked.

Two of the bags dropped and spilled their contents. Julie cursed. "What the fuck? You can't go around creeping up on people like that. Who the hell are you?"

The three of them bent to collect the shopping. Lorne chased an orange and apple into the road, but a passing car squashed them.

"Great, what's the point in buying fresh fruit from the

grocer's? I might as well have bought a plastic bag of them from the supermarket, at least they'd still be intact. I repeat, who are you?"

Sally and Lorne both stood and produced their warrant cards.

"DI Sally Parker and DS Lorne Warner. We're really sorry to have scared you, that wasn't our intention."

"No? Then why do it? Why didn't you call out from a few feet away? It's getting dark now, and you're out here, sneaking up on people, scaring the shit out of them. Where's your common sense? And who's going to pay for the damage? That's what I want to know."

Sally smiled at the woman to try and ease the tension between them. "I'm sorry. I'll get some money from the car to cover the cost."

"Don't be ridiculous. Why is it the police always take people seriously? I'm not that tight or hard up that I can't afford to replace a squished apple and orange. What do you want, anyway?"

"We'd like a chat with you if possible, about your sister."

"Christ, and I didn't think my day could get any worse. How wrong was I!"

Sally inclined her head. "Now you've intrigued me. Can we give you a hand?"

"I think you've done enough damage to my shopping already, but I appreciate the offer. I suppose you'll be wanting a drink, will you? Coppers can't function properly without at least twenty cuppas inside them, can they?"

"We wouldn't want to put you out, but two coffees would be lovely. It's been at least three hours since our last cup, putting a dent in that particular myth concerning the police." Sally grinned.

Julie slotted her key in the lock, pushed the front door

open, and then picked up the last of her shopping. "You'd better come in."

Sally sensed the young woman was about to keep them waiting once they got inside, unpacking her bags a priority rather than leaving the task until they left.

Julie proved her wrong. "I'll make the drinks; I'll sort this lot out later. How do you like your coffee?"

"White with one sugar for both of us, thank you."

"I'll switch the heating on. I don't like to waste money and preheat the house before I get home, not like some of my colleagues, but there are some days I wish I had, like today. I haven't felt warm all day at school, and the heating is really efficient, it has to be for the kids."

"And yet look how many germs get spread at school and taken home to the families," Sally replied. "Can I help? Perhaps pass you the milk out of the fridge?"

"Yes, okay. No, wait, there's only the dregs left of the old one. I'll use the fresh, if it survived the fall."

Sally searched the carriers and found a carton of UHT semi-skimmed and held it up. "Is this it?"

"No, that's for emergencies, in case I can't get out to the shops. There should be a two-pinter in there somewhere."

Lorne took over the search in the bag beside her and held the carton aloft. "Got it."

She handed it to Julie who completed the drinks swiftly.

"Do you want to go through to the lounge or stay in here?"

Sally weighed up the options, considered which room would be warmer until she spotted the boiler at the far end of the room. "Here's fine."

"Very well, have a seat. Will you be wanting a biscuit?"

"Not for us. Thanks very much."

"Take a seat and I'll bring them over."

The kitchen was a little dated but still appeared to be quite modern. Sally suspected it was installed around five to six years earlier. Grey cupboards with a marble-effect splashback that had glints of sparkle in it, unless Sally's eyes were playing tricks on her. The floor had beige stone tiles that had a few cracks here and there. Sally couldn't help wondering if Julie was frequently clumsy, after witnessing her drop the shopping outside.

Julie joined them at the table and handed around the drinks. "You said this was about my sister. What's she been up to now?"

Sally recapped how their morning had panned out, leading up to and including when she and Lorne had taken Zara to hospital, and left it there, intentionally leaving out the conversations they'd had with Julie's parents and brother to see how long it would be before Julie asked.

As it turned out, it wasn't long. "What? She's in hospital? Is she really that bad? Have my parents been informed?"

"Yes, we had to ring them earlier to arrange for them to have Mila for a few days, until your sister is well enough to be discharged."

"My God, how awful. Can you tell me what the prognosis is for her?"

"We can't. I'm going to be brutally honest with you because I believe you're strong enough to hear the truth, unlike your parents. Your sister enforced upon us the need for you all to stay away at this time."

"I don't understand, why?"

"From what I can understand, the doctor seemed to believe that she wouldn't have been with us much longer if we hadn't sought help for her."

Julie stared into her mug and shook her head. She neither glanced up nor spoke for a while. Sally winked at Lorne, sending a silent message that the ploy was deliberate. Lorne gave a brief nod in response, and they both took a sip from their mugs.

Finally, Julie exhaled and said quietly, "I can't believe she nearly died. That is what you're telling me, isn't it?"

"So it would seem. We can sit here and put different spins on it for hours, but it would still amount to the same thing, that your sister was in desperate need of help. That's why Kim called me this morning."

"Jesus, I know Kim. Why the hell didn't she contact me? I would have dropped everything and gone round there."

"Would you? If it came to the crunch?" Sally asked.

"Definitely. Whether we have spoken for two years or not, pushing that aside, she's still my sister." She gasped. "My God, if my sister is in that condition, what about Mila?"

"We're not sure. I suppose if she's not as healthy as she should be, your parents will get in touch once they've picked her up from school." Sally flicked her wrist to check her watch. "I'm assuming they have her by now and she's either gone back home to collect an overnight bag or is settling in at your parents'."

"I should give them a call to check. Will you allow me to do that?"

"You're free to do anything, this is simply an informal chat, however, I'd rather you left it until we've finished."

"Why? Is there any reason? Surely Mila's welfare should be at the forefront of everyone's mind right now, including yours, Inspector."

"You're right, it should be. By all means, make the call."

She quickly reached for her mobile. "Mum, it's me. I've got the police here. They've just gone over what's happened with Zara and told me you've got Mila staying with you for a few days. How is she?"

Sensing something was wrong by the sobbing she could

hear on the other end, Sally asked, "Can you put it on speaker?"

"Sure. Mum, you're not making any sense. The officers can hear what you're saying as you're on speakerphone. What's wrong?"

"When your father went to collect her from school, she was still in the head's office. The school nurse was with her because Mila had passed out. They were sure it was from the shock of hearing the news. They helped your father get Mila in the car. I took one look at her, and I think there's something seriously wrong with her. She's so pale, Julie. I'm worried about her."

"Have you rung the surgery, Mum? Tried to get an emergency appointment with the doctor?"

"Yes, that's the first thing I did. I'm taking her in at nine-thirty in the morning," Amy said between sobs.

"Oh, Mum, that's a relief. How has it come to this? Both of them being ill. It should never have been allowed to happen, ever."

"I know, sweetheart. The guilt won't be easy to shift this time. We should have stuck by Zara, no matter how much she tried to push us away."

"I agree. I'll have a chat with the officers and then come over. Any chance I can have something to eat tonight with you guys?"

"Cottage pie okay for you? There's one in the oven now, and there will be more than enough to go around."

"Sounds delicious. I won't be long. Stay strong in front of Mila. I'm sure she'll be fine with one of your superb meals in her tummy."

"I hope so, love. See you later. Goodbye again, DI Parker."

"Take care, Amy. Will you give me a ring after you've taken Mila to the doctor?"

"I will."

"See you in a little while, Mum. Keep your chin up." Julie ended the call and threw the phone away from her in disgust. "Forgive me for what I'm about to say next, but if that damn sister of mine has put my niece's life in danger, I'm not going to be held responsible for what I do to her. That girl should always come first, not Zara wallowing in self-pity."

"Why don't we hold fire on accusing Zara and find out the facts first?"

"You think I'm blowing this up into something it shouldn't be? Bloody hell, Inspector, you have a lot to learn about what goes on in my sister's head."

"Care to enlighten us?"

"It's always been about her. She was determined to get onto the stage at an early age, used to prance around the house in different costumes. It drove my brother and me nuts... the way our parents let her get away with things, while we got away with nothing."

"Can you give us an example?"

"Christ, how long have you got? I have a whole list of them."

"Ah, anything that stands out from the rest?"

"Yes. One Halloween, my sister went trick or treating on her own, snuck out of the house while Perry and I were getting ready. It was supposed to be a family outing, supervised by the adults. It turned out to be a major search for Zara. All the neighbours helped, neglecting their own kids' excitement, something they had been looking forward to for weeks."

"Oh, that's a shame. I take it you found her?"

"We did. She took off on her own, fancied a walk down by the nearby river, away from all the commotion of the night. Mum should have been livid when a neighbour, who had been walking his dog, persuaded Zara to come back with him. But she wasn't, she was so relieved to have her home. Bloody cheek. If that had been either Perry or me who had wandered off like that, we would have been belted with a strap and forbidden any privileges or outings for a month. Not so for little Miss Goody Two-Shoes, except she was anything but that day. She ended up getting away with it and, in the process, spoilt the night for the other kids on the street. Like I said, she was always the centre of attention."

"What a shame. How did the other kids react?"

"They hated her for it and blamed all of us, not just Zara, but my brother and me as well. That, we couldn't handle. Maybe that was the night the true remorse set in. I've tried and tried to get past it over the years, but it proved to be an impossible undertaking."

"Did you try and thrash things out with Zara? Did she ever sit you down and ask you why you had so much resentment towards her?"

"No. That proves how thick-skinned she is, though, doesn't it?"

"I'm not a psychiatrist, I couldn't possibly comment on what goes on in a person's mind. I prefer to deal with the facts and, after having a conversation with your sister yesterday, she appeared to be a very confused soul, lacking in self-worth and confidence. Maybe it's time for you all to start afresh."

Julie wagged her finger and pursed her lips. "See, here we go again. What you're effectively telling me, or my family, to do, is forget about what went on in the past and look to a brighter future, except it will be down to us to be the ones to change our ways, not Zara."

"I'm saying nothing of the sort and wouldn't dream of assuming this is going to be simple to put right. What I believe in, is giving someone in desperate need a second chance. And yes, I appreciate Zara is the one who is crying out for the attention she's lacked from her family over the years."

Julie pointed at her. "There you go. You said you prefer to deal with the facts as they come your way, you've just said it yourself... and sorry, that doesn't wash with me. All we're going to be doing over the coming weeks, if we accept her back into the fold, is run around after her again, as usual. She'll be rubbing her hands in glee."

Sally tutted and then sighed. "We've just visited your brother, and he's pretty much said the same thing."

"And yet we've not discussed my sister for a while. It's extremely hard to forgive and forget for some people. Especially those who were treated badly as a result of someone else's actions."

"I can understand that. We're not here to judge, all we're aware of is the facts, and they're clearly prominent in our minds, having seen your sister this morning."

"Bearing in mind we haven't met Mila yet," Lorne added.

Sally raised her thumb at her partner. "I agree. And if your mother is that concerned about Mila to have contacted the doctor's for an emergency appointment, then maybe it's time to call a truce with your sister. What do you think?"

There was a moment's silence. Julie picked at the skin around her thumb on her right hand. "I'm going to hold back from committing either way until I see for myself what condition my niece is in. So, intrigue is getting the better of me now. Why are you here, the real reason?"

Sally cleared her throat, anticipating a backlash from Julie. "Because we've decided to reinvestigate the disappearance of your brother-in-law."

Julie slammed back in her chair. "What the fuck? Why?"

"I'm doing a favour for Kim. Saying that, having read the file from the initial investigation, there are genuine gaps that we're keen to explore."

"What sort of gaps?" she asked, perplexed.

"Well, for a start, we need to know why Christian went missing and how. There's very little camera footage that should have been followed up."

"You know what that would tell me? That it was planned."

Cocking an eyebrow, Sally asked, "Care to share what you mean by that statement?"

"Perry and I are of the same opinion, that his disappearance was a little too convenient."

"You think he's started up somewhere else with the money he obtained from the loans?"

"Don't you? Maybe you should spend your time searching for the truth on that angle."

"It's something we're delving into back at the station. Don't worry, we'll dig deep, we always do."

"Good, I'm glad to hear it."

"What about the loans? When did you first learn about them?"

"At the same time as everyone else in the family, a few days after he went missing. A coincidence maybe, but I'm not convinced. I don't want to say anything more about my sister, I think it will lead to clouding your judgement about me. What I will say is there has to be a connection. According to Zara, she swore blind at the time that she wasn't aware the loans existed. I find that incredibly hard to believe."

"And what if, as she suspected, Christian forged her signature?"

Julie closed her eyes and shrugged. When she opened them again, she stared at Sally and said, "Maybe that's why I chose to be a teacher and not a police officer."

Sally frowned. "I don't understand."

"I think she's pulling the wool over everyone's eyes, including yours."

"I can't believe that."

"Why?"

"Because of the 'slum' she is living in. If fraud was on the agenda, it hasn't paid off. What about Christian? Why would he run off? That is what you suspect, isn't it?"

Julie closed her eyes again.

"Why would he run off if she's tried to defraud the loan companies?" Sally asked.

Julie held her hands up and slapped them on the table. "I can't answer that. Maybe the truth is hidden in there somewhere and it's up to you to uncover it, if you can. All respect to you, because as a family, we've never been able to figure out what's going on in that head of Zara's."

"And that's why, as a family, you felt the need to cut her off, because you believed she was deceiving you?"

"Perhaps. Speaking for Perry and myself, we had a rough childhood and found the situation untenable when the loan demands started dropping on her doormat. Our sister never stopped buying, whether at the shops or online. Look where that got her. If I recall rightly, she lost her home, her business and her husband, all in the space of three months."

"And, in your eyes, that was no one else's fault but her own?"

"I don't know. Nothing is ever clear cut where Zara is concerned. I don't know how many more times I have to tell you that. Please, all I'm asking is that you don't take too much notice of her tales of woe. Get sucked into her fantasy world, if you like."

"I'm sorry, it's hard not to, given the state we found her in this morning. A terrifying condition that the doctors felt needed assessing right away, otherwise she wouldn't have been admitted."

"Whatever. She's always known how far to push it, that's all I'm saying."

"So, you believe it was her intention to nearly starve herself to death to get back in your family's good books."

"Starve herself?"

"I told you, another few days and she would no longer be with us."

Her head dropped, and then Sally spotted a tear seep onto Julie's cheek. Lorne nudged Sally's knee under the table.

"I'm sorry," Julie said. "My anger has gone through the roof over the years. You have no idea of the torment my brother and I have had to put up with, feeling like outcasts in our family because all the attention flowed in our sister's direction."

"I'm sorry you were subjected to that during your childhood. Perry said the same. He also mentioned that since Zara has been out of the picture your parents have been different towards you both. Maybe you should discuss what it'll mean to have Zara back in your lives and talk through your concerns."

"Maybe. I think we have different priorities that need to be dealt with, knowing what lies ahead of Zara and Mila. This is such a mess. You have to admit it's selfish on my sister's part."

Sally shrugged. "I don't know her well enough to believe that to be true. All I can reiterate is that Zara has reached out for help. That must have taken a lot of guts for her to do after all that has gone on between you all in the past."

Julie shook her head. "She didn't reach out to us, not directly. And why did she leave it so long? If she was in dire straits, shouldn't she have swallowed her pride and asked her family for help?"

"Pride and fear of rejection will stop most people from trying to make amends for what has gone on in their past. Please, give her a chance."

"Don't put the onus on my shoulders, Inspector. All I can

do is promise that, as a family, we'll discuss where we go from here. My concern lies with my poor niece, who I perceive to be an innocent party in all of this, and how much this is going to affect her mental status, on top of having to deal with what happened to her father. Which still remains a total mystery."

"I agree. I think both Zara and her daughter have needlessly suffered since his mysterious disappearance. Whether that was down to Zara remains to be seen. What we're here for today is to ask you some questions about the time all this kicked off. Can I ask you to cast your mind back to before you saw Christian for the last time? Was there anything suspicious going on in either his or Zara's life that you can put your finger on?"

Julie mulled the question over while she sipped at her coffee. "I don't think so, no. I feel I must add that we were never that close, so they wouldn't have confided in me if there was anything untoward going on. So, it's a bit of a pointless exercise you showing up here if only to ask me that."

Sally nodded. "Okay, does that mean you're going to give me the same response regarding the business as well?"

"Even more so. I kept my nose well and truly out of that, not my bag at all."

"In that case, I believe our job here is done."

"Sorry I couldn't be of more help in the circumstances. Do you want to leave me a card? Something might come to mind after you leave."

"Of course." Sally slid one across the table to her, then she and Lorne took another sip from their coffee and stood. "We'll see ourselves out, leave you to deal with your shopping."

Julie smiled for the first time since they'd met her. "Thanks. Good luck with your investigation, I hope it leads somewhere this time. I think it's the not knowing that can be destructive, don't you? Maybe that's what has happened in this case, Zara's plodded on in the past and finally it's suddenly hit her and had a devastating effect. Did she tell you if anything had triggered what's going on with her now?"

"No, she hasn't been able to give us any insight at all. Thanks for speaking with us today, sorry we got off on the wrong foot."

Julie waved Sally's concern away. "It was the straw that broke the camel's back. I had a very frustrating day at work and was kicking myself for needing to do the shopping on the way home. It's one chore I detest most in the world."

Sally smiled. "Can't say I'm overly keen on it either. Take care."

They jumped back into their vehicle and returned to the station, both wrapped up in their own thoughts.

Sally climbed the stairs to the office on weary legs. "I'm done in. I can't recall ever feeling this tired on the first day of a case. How are you holding up?"

"I'm okay. Can't say I'm allowing it to affect me that much. It's obvious you're getting involved in it, though."

"I think I've surprised myself today, the emotions this has stirred up already. All I will say is thank God Kim got in touch with me when she did, otherwise the investigation might have taken a different direction."

"You're not kidding."

"We'll go through what the team have come up with in our absence and then go home. I'm going to make some notes tonight, I feel I need to."

"You think we've missed something obvious?" Lorne frowned.

"There's something playing havoc with my gut. Maybe I just need to get a good night's sleep to put everything back into perspective again."

"I agree. We should revisit a couple of aspects of the investigation in the morning, maybe split the team up to cover the interviews. The quicker we get those out of the way the better."

"That definitely needs to be a priority."

# CHAPTER 6

The following morning, Sally decided to head into work early. Her first job was to contact Lorne to see if she wanted to join her.

"You read my mind. Let's do it."

Sally swung by Lorne's house ten minutes later, both eager to get on with their day.

"Tell me you managed to get some rest last night and weren't up working until all hours."

"I wasn't and yes, surprisingly sleep came easily last night. What about you?"

Lorne grinned. "I always sleep well, compared to the days when I was in charge."

"Sounds about right. I'm counting down the days to my retirement, and believe me, I won't make the same mistake you made."

"Charming. It only happened the three times… hang on, or was it four? No, I think it might have been five."

They both laughed.

"Your indecisiveness knows no bounds, Lorne Warner.

The only thing I know is that this time around I'm the one benefitting from having you by my side."

"Now don't go getting all soppy on me. I wonder what delights today will bring."

"Hopefully some form of leads we can chase up. Quite frankly, it's not looking good, is it?"

"Remaining positive can only work in our favour."

THE REST of the team arrived around their normal time, and Sally held the morning meeting once Lorne had supplied them all with coffees.

"As you can see from the board, there's not much to go on as yet, which is frustrating the hell out of me. What we've established so far is that there appears to be a huge rift between the siblings. We are all aware how detrimental envy can be—whether that's something we should prioritise, the jury is still out for me. What Lorne and I witnessed yesterday was that we spoke to five family members, and their emotions were all visible and easy to assess. We don't have the answers yet, and to be honest with you, I'm not sure if any are ever going to come our way. The positive side to what we've achieved is that Zara is in hospital getting the care and treatment she needs to put her life back together, and I think we've done enough with the family to make them sit up and consider if the falling-out they've had has been worth it. I know the parents have huge regrets and are trying to make amends by caring for their granddaughter during her mother's spell in hospital." She paused and perched on the desk behind her. "The sister and brother, well, only time will tell if they can find it within themselves to forgive and forget and show Zara the compassion she needs to get through this. I'm not altogether hopeful about that, are you, Lorne?"

"Yeah, I'm not convinced about it either. Perry and Julie, without speaking to each other, both gave us the same account of what they've had to deal with growing up in that household. The bitterness is still extensive, in my opinion."

"I agree. One thing that puzzles me is that the pair have never fallen out with their parents, not as such. Their anger and frustration appears to have always been directed at Zara. If you turn that on its head, that's a lot of emotional angst for Zara to have dealt with, along with what else was going on in her life, her husband's disappearance. So, where do we begin today? Jordan, have you finished compiling the list of friends we need to speak with?"

"I think it's complete now. Only one main friend on Christian's side. He barely used Facebook to keep the world up to date with what was going on in his life, unlike Zara. Her list, in comparison, is vast."

Sally cringed. "How vast are we talking here?"

"Off the top of my head, I reckon fifteen to twenty names."

"That's more than I anticipated, but if we can split it up, we should be able to get through everyone quickly throughout the day. Are you all up for it?"

The team all nodded in agreement.

"Okay, I'll leave you to deal with that, Jordan. Has anyone uncovered anything else while going over the background searches?"

"Very little in all honesty, boss," Joanna said. "Does that surprise me? I'm not so sure. If they were busy people, running a business, all their time would be concentrated on that side of things, wouldn't it?"

"I agree. Any bad press for the dance studio via the social media platforms?" Sally asked.

"I haven't discovered anything in that vein so far."

"That's one less angle for us to need to check then. So,

we'll concentrate all our efforts on interviewing the friends, if they're easily traceable after all this time. Let me know how you're getting on and when we can get started on it. I'll be in my office, doing the usual." She left the team and entered her office. One glance outside the window told her that the weather was matching her mood of doom and gloom.

The post held the usual mundane start to her day. Determined to get any post that had been hanging around for a week or more out of the way, she didn't raise her head for another hour. When she did, it was to answer a call that had been put through to her.

"DI Sally Parker, how may I help?"

"Sorry to interrupt, Inspector, it's Amy Walters here. You asked me to give you an update after Mila visited the doctor."

"Ah yes, hello, Amy. How are things going between you all?"

"We were really concerned about Mila last night. We dragged another mattress into the spare room, and I ended up sleeping on that for the night, close to her."

"Ouch, sorry to hear that. Did she sleep at all? What did the doctor have to say?"

"We've had little to no sleep. I knew there was something seriously wrong with Mila the second I laid eyes on her."

"Serious? What are we talking about, Amy?"

"Kidney failure. It's been going on for months, so the doctor said."

"Jesus. Where is she now?"

"I'm at the hospital with her. They're trying to get her sorted as a matter of urgency. Zara should have taken her daughter to the doctor long ago. She hasn't. Neither of them had seen a doctor in well over a year, and now… look where they both are."

"This is devastating news. I'm going to come to the hospital, see if there's anything I can do to speed things along for you."

"Thank you. I don't mind telling you that I feel like I'm drowning at the moment. My head is in a total spin. I don't know what to do for the best."

"Right now, all you can do is be there for Mila. I'll get on the road straight away. I'll see you soon. Where are you?"

"Still in triage. They're trying to sort out an emergency bed for her, but it's taking forever."

"Hang in there. We'll try and hurry things along when we get there. Is Mila awake? Responsive to what's going on around her?"

"She's coping well, far better than I am. But I can see how worried she is, it's there, in her eyes."

"She's bound to be anxious, it's only natural. Try to keep your anguish hidden from her if you can."

"I'll try."

"Is your husband with you?" The line fell silent. "Amy? Are you still there?"

"Yes, I'm here. Umm… rather than sit around here, Leslie thought he'd go and see how Zara is getting on."

*Shit! She doesn't want that.* "Ah, I thought we agreed to leave her alone, at her request."

"You don't know my husband, Inspector. Once his mind is made up about something, there's no stopping him."

"Okay, well, there's not much we can do to change things now. I'll see you soon." Sally slammed the phone down in disgust and shot out of the office. "Lorne, we're needed at the hospital ASAP."

Lorne immediately jumped to her feet and gasped. "No, it's not Zara, is it?"

"No, I'll fill you in on the way. While we're out, guys, I'm going to need you to divvy up the list. Once you've traced all the names, get out there. We need to hit this thick and fast now. Joanna, you're going to need to stay behind and man the phones. Jordan and Stuart, if you can find a couple of people to question this morning and leave Joanna to source the details of the rest, she can relay the information to you whilst you're out on the road. Sorry, that's the best I can come up with at this time. Lorne, we need to go. Are you ready?"

"Of course."

They ran down the steps and out to the car. Lorne knew better than to hassle her until the journey was underway.

"What's going on?"

"Zara's not the only one who is in hospital now. Mila was admitted this morning with kidney failure. Amy just rang me to let me know."

"Fuck, that's all we need. How bad is she?"

"Bad enough. It turns out that neither mother nor daughter have visited a doctor in a while."

"Jesus, this is crap, Sal. I haven't visited the doctor for a while—no, wait, yes, I have, for HRT—but before that, you don't want to waste their time if there's nothing wrong with you, but it's a different ballgame if you're bloody sick. What was Zara thinking?"

"That's not all. Amy and her husband are at the hospital with Mila. Amy told me that her husband had gone off to visit Zara."

"Shit, damn and blast! Exactly what she doesn't need or want. What is wrong with that man?"

Sally sighed and hitched up a shoulder. "I have no idea what's running through his mind, but I can sense how damaging this scenario is going to be. Why don't folks let things lie? Allow the dust to settle? Take things slowly?"

"Pass. His actions could have a severe impact on Zara's health, especially if he starts having a go at her."

"Hopefully it won't come to that. To say I'm livid would

be an understatement, that's why I told Amy that we'd pay them a visit right away."

"I don't blame you. What about Mila? How desperate is her condition?"

"We're about to find out. I thought our being there, showing our support to the family, would help, maybe hurry things along a little."

"It can't hurt."

WHEN IT WAS CONVENIENT, Sally put her foot down on the country roads leading to Norwich, which meant they arrived ten minutes earlier than anticipated.

She pulled into the car park and listened to Lorne let out a relieved sigh. "Sorry, was that too scary for you?"

"And some. I think I've broken half a dozen nails clinging to my seat."

Sally laughed. "Your exaggeration levels go up and down like a damn yo-yo. Come on, time is marching on."

"No shit!"

They raced through the corridor to triage, and Sally flashed her ID at the same receptionist she had spoken to the day before.

"Mila Starr was rushed in this morning. Her grandparents are with her. Any chance we can see her, please?"

"Ah, yes. I know the patient. Take a seat. I'll need to make a phone call first, but there's something important I have to deal with before I get around to that."

"Umm… it'll only take a moment for you to push a buzzer to let us in. We can sort out the rest on the other side." Sally smiled at the young receptionist. Who then reached to her left and hit the button.

"If I get into trouble for this, I'll expect you to speak up for me."

"Thanks, just send them my way."

"I don't know how you get away with it," Lorne mumbled as they tore towards the door and slipped into the triage area.

"There's Amy, up ahead."

Mrs Walters saw them tearing up the corridor towards them and broke down in tears. Sally gathered her in her arms, held Amy for a few moments, and then guided her to the nearby chair.

"Hey, what's all this?"

"It's the pressure. I'm struggling to deal with it all. This time a few days ago the only concern I had was what I was going to cook for our evening meal. Now look at the situation we're in. Both my daughter and granddaughter in hospital with life-threatening conditions." Her hands covered her face, and she sobbed.

Sally flung an arm around her shoulders, her heart breaking for the poor woman. Lorne sat on the other side, looking dumbstruck.

In the distance, Sally saw the depressed figure of Leslie Walters coming towards them. His steps quickened once he realised his wife was upset.

"What's going on? Is it Mila?" he demanded, a few feet away from his wife.

"No, she's okay. I mean, she's settled and they're dealing with her, but she's far from fine. Why did you take off like that? I told you not to go and see Zara, but you pushed me aside, as usual. Not giving two hoots about what I'm dealing with at this time."

"Don't start, Amy. You have no idea what I've just witnessed." His gaze drifted to Sally, and he shook his head. "You should have warned us."

Amy's gaze shifted between Sally and her husband.

"I passed on her message that she didn't want to see either of you. That's all I could do."

"What's going on?" Amy demanded. "Someone has to tell me. I'm her mother, for Christ's sake, I have a right to know."

"The best way I can describe it is that our daughter is…" He paused, obviously grappling for the right words.

"Don't do this," Sally pleaded. "She's in the best place, receiving the care she needs, leave it at that for now."

"Not good enough, Inspector. My wife deserves to know."

"Then tell me, Leslie," Amy whispered.

"It's horrendous, love. It took me a while to recognise her. She's in an absolutely appalling state. Her skin hanging off her bones. No meat on her at all. It's like something out of one of those war films, you know, the Pathé News, showing all the men at Belsen and the other prisoner of war camps."

Amy's face creased up again. "No, I can't take any more of this, I just can't. The guilt flowing through me is off the scale. How did our once-loving family descend to this? How could she allow herself to get into that state? And that's without considering what she's done to Mila in there. That sweet innocent child deserved to be treated better by her mother. I'm not sure I'll ever be able to forgive her now. She's selfish to the core, pure and simple, for what she's done to them."

"Please, try not to be too hard on her," Sally said. "Your daughter has had the worst of times to contend with whilst trying her best to raise a teenager."

"Without support," Leslie added. "Go on, that is what you were about to say next, isn't it? You think we're to blame, not Zara, don't you?"

Sally shrugged. "Not my field of expertise. I'm not in the blame game business, sir."

"The underlying feeling is there, I can see it in your eyes. We had no control over this situation, and I refuse to accept any responsibility for it."

"You have that right. I don't believe going over the same ground will prove beneficial to either of you. Why don't you take my seat, care for your wife, and I'll try and find out what's going on with Mila?"

Reluctantly, he swapped places with Sally. Lorne got into step beside Sally as they searched the corridor for the doctor.

"Hey, you're going to need to calm down before you speak to anyone," Lorne warned.

"I'm fine. Pissed off that he went against his own daughter's wishes. It's as though she doesn't have a say in what happens to her. To me, that's disrespectful."

"I suppose we need to take a step back, assess the situation from both points of view. Their only grandchild is seriously ill in hospital. He probably visited Zara with the intention of getting some answers and what he witnessed shocked him to another level."

"We can make excuses for him all day long, Lorne, the fact is, I feel let down by his actions, which is nothing in comparison to what Zara must be going through right now. She must be bloody mortified, and I bet she's blaming me for telling her parents."

"At the end of the day, she can't do that. She involved them by asking them to look after Mila, you didn't. If your child was in hospital and told you to keep away, then surely inquisitiveness would get the better of you sooner or later, wouldn't it?"

A doctor came out of a room ahead of them before Sally could respond.

"Hello, Doctor," Sally shouted, "do you have a moment?"

The man turned to face them and closed the file he was holding. "How can I help?"

Sally produced her warrant card. "DI Sally Parker, and my partner, DS Lorne Warner. I was wondering if we could have a chat with you about Mila Starr."

He pointed at the room behind him. "Okay, let's do it in my office." Once settled at his desk, he asked, "What is it you want to know?"

"How she is. What her prognosis is."

He inhaled a breath and steepled his fingers under his chin. "To be perfectly honest with you, the prognosis isn't very good. We're carrying out a lot of tests on her at present, which will hopefully give us a better indication of what we're dealing with. The truth is, the young lady has been ill for quite a while but hasn't sought any medical help. Whether that is down to her ignoring her illness or whether it's down to neglectful parenting, I'm not sure we're ever going to find out the truth."

"You can't tell us what her chances are?" Sally asked, shocked by the news.

"I'm not prepared to commit to anything of that nature at this time. It's our priority to continue with the tests, draw a conclusion from them instead of using guesswork, and we'll go from there."

"What's the worst-case scenario?"

"That she dies. Nevertheless, we will do everything we can to prevent that, of course. We need a day or two to keep assessing her. She needs a break, or her body does, between the tests."

"Sad though it's a desperate situation, or is that overstating things?"

"I think you've pretty much nailed it with that assessment. Now, if you'll excuse me, I really need to get on." He rose from his seat and motioned for them to leave as he held the door open.

"Thank you for seeing us. If I leave you a card, will you ring me as soon as you know anything concrete about what her treatment is likely to be?"

"You can, but I can't promise anything. It's the family who

have the right to know any outcome, not the police, unless you're telling me this is a police matter?"

"No, it's not. Thanks for speaking with us."

He nodded and went on his way.

Sally faced the wall and rested her forehead against it. "Shit! That poor girl."

Lorne rubbed Sally's arm. "Admittedly, it doesn't sound good. We're going to need to remain positive."

Sally turned around and glanced up and down the corridor. "So which was it? Mila brushing over how ill she was or a case of Zara not seeking the treatment her daughter needed?"

Lorne shrugged. "Take your pick. In Zara's defence, I know what a challenge it can be bringing up a teenager, and that was ten to fifteen years ago. I reckon it's far worse for parents nowadays."

"I guess we'll have to wait and see, it's too late to worry about that now. But he's just told us Mila could die, so she must have been in agony for a long time, mustn't she?"

"You're asking the wrong person. I haven't got a clue about kidney disease or failure. Maybe she had other symptoms and dismissed them, thinking it was something else."

"Possibly. Christ, what I find inconceivable is that she could die from this. She's sixteen and should be out there, looking forward to what lies ahead of her. Making plans for what career she intends to have in the future. Instead, she's lying in a hospital bed, seriously ill."

"Why don't we go and see how Zara is? You can visit her while I try and do some research online. I don't know enough about the condition to be able to give you any guidance on it, not that you're asking me to."

"Good idea. I'm as much in the dark about this as you are. It'll be good to brush up on it, if only to know what to expect. I felt the doctor was being a bit cagey with us."

"We caught him on the hop."

"That's true."

They set off up the corridor and wound their way through the hospital to Zara's room.

"I'll take a seat out here and search the internet, see what I can come up with."

"Thanks, Lorne. Wish me luck."

Lorne held up her crossed fingers.

Feeling apprehensive, unsure how the visit was going to pan out, Sally lightly knocked on the door and entered. Zara opened her eyes and smiled weakly.

"How are you doing?" Sally rested a hand on Zara's.

"Not so bad. I would be feeling better if my father hadn't dropped by to see me. I wasn't expecting to see him and hadn't prepared myself for his visit. It must have been a shock for him to have seen me like this."

"I'm sorry, I passed on your wishes not to be disturbed. Your mother appears to have accepted your decision, but the same couldn't be said for your father."

She raised a hand. "Don't blame yourself, I know how stubborn and determined my father can be."

Sally returned the smile and dropped into the chair beside Zara. "Are you up for having a chat?"

"I think so. I sense what's coming next. You want to discuss Mila and what's going on with her, don't you?"

"Yes, I think we should."

"She told me a few weeks ago that she was having problems with going to the toilet. I tried to get a doctor's appointment for her, but you know how stressful that can be. I rang every morning for a week, and the receptionist told me they were only taking on emergency appointments. So, I left it. I know now that was the wrong thing to do and I'll never forgive myself for not being more forceful under the circumstances."

"I get that, you were suffering yourself at the time. I'm sorry the system has let you both down. Why didn't you come straight to A and E to seek the help you needed?"

"Because I wasn't brought up that way. In my eyes, A and E is for when you're bleeding out, having a heart attack, or in excruciating pain. It's laughable to see people using it as a kind of drop-in centre for minor ailments. That's putting an unnecessary strain on the NHS. I thought I was doing the right thing, but it appears to have backfired on both of us."

"You could say that. Still, there's no point reproaching yourself. How was your father towards you?"

"Hard to say. I think mixed emotions were running through him. Anger being the most prominent to begin with. After scolding me for a few minutes, he appeared to reassess the situation and calm down a bit. That's when the remorse kicked in, at least I think it was remorse. There might have been an added dose of guilt in there as well."

"I hope it wasn't too uncomfortable for you?"

"It was passable. I think he could tell that I didn't have any fight left in me. He's livid about Mila, but there's little I can do about that now. Like me, she's in the best place for her. Hopefully they'll get her sorted and back home soon."

"Let's hope you'll both be back on your feet within the next few days." *Believe that and you'll believe anything. Your recovery is going to take months, Zara. How could you have let yourself get this bad?*

"We'll see. I think I feel more positive about it than I did yesterday. Everyone has been so nice to me; they haven't judged me in the slightest."

"That's wonderful to hear. The staff have always been helpful to us whenever we've had to pay someone a visit. So, have they told you what the next step is for you?"

"My psych assessment went okay. They told me they don't feel there's a need to section me, which was a relief.

They've also told me to expect to stay in hospital for the next ten to fourteen days. My overriding fear is what will happen to me when I'm discharged."

"If things progress and go well with your parents, maybe you could move in with them for a few months, just until you really get back on your feet. I got the impression they would be open to that suggestion. Would it be something you'd consider?"

"I don't know. I'd have to seriously think about it. It's not easy relinquishing your independence at the drop of a hat. There's obviously still some conflict between us. In all honesty, I'm not sure what would be the best way forward."

"Well, fortunately, you don't have to make that decision yet."

Zara sighed, and her eyes closed. Before long, her breathing had changed, and Sally knew it was time for her to leave. She crept out of the room. Zara didn't stir.

"Everything all right in there?" Lorne asked.

Sally sank into the chair beside her and leaned her head back against the wall. "I think so. She seemed pretty relaxed about her father's visit but mortified that she'd let Mila down."

"Understandable. Did she try and seek help for her daughter, or didn't she know what was going on?"

"Mila complained she was ill a few weeks ago. Zara tried her very best to get her in to see the doctor, but it proved useless. This was the result. Anyway, how did you get on?"

Sally could tell by the expression on her partner's face that the news wasn't going to be good.

"Far from ideal. If she was suffering from kidney disease, the prognosis isn't too bad. Saying that, kidney failure is a different kettle of fish altogether."

"Ouch, now you're worrying me. Go on, hit me with it."

"The way forward is whether they think she'll respond to dialysis or not."

"And if she doesn't?"

"Then the only other option on the cards is a kidney transplant, and not everyone is a good match."

"Jesus, let's hope the dialysis wins that argument. I still wouldn't relish going down that route. What if she needs a transplant?"

"They carry out tests on family members first. If there are no matches, then she'll be put on the waiting list."

"Still touch and go then?"

"So it would seem."

"Sod it. Not what I was hoping would be the outcome at all."

"A word of caution, if I may?"

Sally nodded.

"I wouldn't say anything to the grandparents, let the doctor be the one to tell them."

"Suits me. Let's hope Google is wrong with the advice it's dishing out this time. We'd better get back to the Walters, they'll be wondering what's going on if we're gone too long."

"How are you going to play it with them?"

They set off.

"Like everything else at the moment, I'm going to wing it."

They both laughed.

IT TOOK a while to convince the Walters that the blame didn't lie at Zara's door for Mila's circumstances, and after a few minutes debating the critical evidence Sally had produced, on Zara's behalf, they agreed. Sally relayed the information the doctor had divulged and told them that they would be the first to be consulted regarding Mila's assessment. Then

Sally had excused herself and Lorne and driven back to the station.

On the way they picked up lunch for the rest of the team. Jordan and Stuart were still out when they arrived. Joanna told them they had spoken to several of Zara's friends during the morning, none of whom could shed any light on anything they didn't already know.

Ravenous, Sally tucked into her tuna and sweetcorn sandwich and contemplated which direction the investigation should take next.

"Anything pertinent showing up to do with the dance studio via SM, Joanna?"

"I found one minor complaint about the dance studio's heating cutting out during one session, that's all."

Sally rolled her eyes. "Idiots! Christ, if you can't keep warm during a workout, there's no hope, is there?"

The three of them laughed.

It was several hours before Jordan and Stuart returned to the station. Sally could tell how frustrated they were by the way they flopped into their chairs.

"Rough day, guys?" Sally asked.

"The pits. Not even a glimmer of something we could latch on to, boss," Jordan said.

"Don't let it get you down, something is bound to come our way soon. Have you eaten?"

"No, we ploughed on, regardless. Didn't want to let you down."

"Nonsense, you've never let me down in the past. There are some sandwiches for you both over at the drinks station. No one is going to blame you for feeling disappointed. You tried your best, that's all that counts."

"But where do we go from here?" Lorne asked.

"I wish I knew. We'll continue going through the friends'

list. Did you get around to speaking with any of Christian's friends, Jordan?"

"No, the one we had a note of proved to be elusive."

Sally inclined her head. "As in you think he was avoiding you?"

"Hard to say. He works in a factory. One minute he was free to speak with us, the next he wasn't. We hung around in the reception area for fifteen minutes, only to be told that he'd left the building on an emergency."

"Interesting. Okay, let's revisit him tomorrow, Lorne and I will take that on. Sounds like something is amiss to me."

"We thought the same," Jordan replied.

Sally stretched her arms above her head. "I'm done in. We've chased our tails around the block a few times again today, I think we should call it quits…" As if on cue, the phone in her office rang. She tutted and ran to answer it. "It never fails, does it?" She answered the phone on the fifth ring. "Hello, DI Sally Parker, how can I help?"

"Ah, I was just about to hang up. It's Doctor Bussell at the hospital, Inspector. We met earlier."

Sally dropped into her chair. By his tone, she sensed the news was about to turn her day upside down. "Ah, yes, hello, Doctor. How is Mila doing?"

"Not good, not good at all. I thought my prognosis was on the cautious side, but I had to make sure before I revealed the true extent of the damage."

"Sounds ominous. Is she dying?"

"I'm hopeful we'll be able to intervene before it comes to that. She's a very, very sick young lady. If we step in quickly, we might, only might, be able to save her."

"Jesus, not the news I was expecting to hear. Is there anything I can do to help?"

"I'm not sure. I was hoping that you might be in the best position to be of assistance."

"Name it. I'll do what I can."

"I think we're past the stage where we can only offer dialysis. That means a transplant is her only hope of surviving."

Sally cast her mind back to the article Lorne had sourced on the internet and gulped. "Umm...what's the process with that?"

"We're going to run some tests, check if any of her immediate family are a match. If not, she'll need to go on the waiting list."

Sally shook her head and closed her eyes, wishing she could have blocked out that news. "Dare I ask how long the list is?"

"I'd rather not say, I find it all too depressing. There's been a recent change in the organ donation scheme, however, it's still not made the impact we thought it would."

"Like everything in this life, I suppose the kinks need to be ironed out first."

"Exactly. We've already taken the samples we need from the grandparents, and Zara's brother and sister are coming in to give us a sample within the hour."

"That's good of them. I thought they might be reluctant to pitch in."

"I believe they took a fair bit of convincing. Of course, the ideal candidate would be a parent. With Zara's health issues, I don't think that's a viable prospect at all. Hence the reason I'm calling you."

"The father?"

"Yes. The grandparents informed me that he went missing a couple of years ago and that you've recently reopened the investigation into his disappearance. Have you got anywhere with that?"

"Nothing so far." A lightbulb went off in Sally's mind. "Nevertheless, if he's out there, this might be the ideal time to bring him in from the cold."

"I'll leave that up to you. I just thought you'd want to know how to proceed. I'm going to have to go now."

"Thanks for the update, Doc. How long have we got?"

"A few days to a week, tops."

"Shit! Okay, leave it with me." She ended the call and contacted Georgia Neves right away.

"Hello, Georgia Neves speaking."

"Georgia, long time no hear. It's DI Sally Parker."

"Oh, hello, stranger. How's it going over on the Cold Case Team?"

"Not so good with the new case we've taken on. I'm hoping that will change after I've spoken with you."

"Go on. You know if I can help, I'll do my very best for you. What do you need?"

Sally explained the dire situation filling her week and hoped against hope that Georgia gave her the response she was after. "Well, what do you think? In your opinion, will it be worth putting out a conference?"

"Hey, who knows? It's got to be worth a shot if his daughter's life is in danger, hasn't it? I don't want to know the ins and outs behind his disappearance, but if he is still around and hasn't been bumped off, then surely, he'd want to do the right thing, wouldn't he?"

"That's what I'm hoping. Okay, I know it's late now, can you make the arrangements in the morning?"

"Absolutely. Leave it with me. Are there any times you need to avoid tomorrow?"

"Nothing yet. There's someone we need to track down urgently first thing, but the rest of the day is clear."

"I'll get back to you by nine-thirty at the latest."

"You're amazing. It's always a pleasure speaking with you, Georgia."

"And you're such a creep, Sally Parker. Enjoy your evening."

"I'll try. I'm bound to be distracted by what's happened today."

"Bless you. I don't know how you manage to leave your work behind you when you're confronted with such devastating news. Let's see if we can do the right thing for Zara and her daughter. Hopefully, if her father is still around, his conscience will prick him into action and that will be the problem solved."

"Let's hope so. Thanks, matey. Speak soon." Sally hung up and stared at the wall ahead of her, her mind stirring up a whirlwind of possibilities. None of which seemed guaranteed in their outcome, only hopeful. Sally made a few notes and then joined the others. "Georgia is going to try and arrange a press conference for the morning. I think we should leave it there for the day and start over tomorrow."

## CHAPTER 7

"Right, I've heard back from Georgia. She's organised the conference for midday. That gives us the morning to visit Paul Collins," Sally informed Lorne after she'd dropped into her office with a top-up of coffee.

"When do you want to set off?" Lorne pointed at the paperwork littering Sally's desk. "Before you tackle that lot or after?"

Sally raised an eyebrow and smiled. "What do you reckon? Needs must, eh?"

"I'll get my jacket."

Lorne left the room, and Sally picked up the notebook in which she'd made copious notes the evening before, at home, much to Simon's annoyance, then followed her partner.

THE FACTORY WAS SITUATED on the outskirts of Mulbarton. The car park was half-empty. Sally reversed into the first available spot she could find, closest to the main entrance. "Are you ready for every eventuality?"

"I am. I have my spray in my pocket."

Sally leaned over and extracted the Taser from the glove box she had signed out before they'd left the station. "This should put a stop to him eluding us this time."

"The A-team to the rescue."

"Now, now, the boys did their best."

The receptionist was busy shuffling papers and glanced up as they approached the desk. "Hello. Can I help?"

Sally showed her warrant card. "DI Sally Parker and DS Lorne Warner. We're here to speak with Paul Collins if he's available. A couple of our colleagues dropped by yesterday but, unfortunately, Mr Collins was called away on an emergency."

"Ah, yes. Strange, that was. He's back in today. I'll give him a bell, see if he can see you."

"I'd rather you take us straight to him. We wouldn't want to miss him again, you know, two days on the trot."

"Well, that's usually against the firm's policy. He works on the factory floor. I might need to run it past the line manager first."

"I'm not averse to that."

The receptionist left her desk and made the call on the other side of the room. She returned and said, "He's given us the all-clear. If you'd like to follow me, ladies?"

Their footsteps echoed down the hallway. The receptionist took them to a large noisy room, full of staff wearing white uniforms.

"You'll need to put on the protective clothing before we go any further. In here."

She took them into a locker room where they pulled on white coats, before they continued on their journey. She introduced them to Frank Tyrell, the line manager, who showed them into his office. A man in his late thirties was standing by the window. He glanced over his shoulder and eyed them with concern as they entered the room.

"I'll leave you to get acquainted," Tyrell said. "I can only spare him for a maximum of fifteen minutes. I hope that will be enough for you. We're on a tight deadline. If the goods aren't packed up and in the warehouse by ten, we could all lose our jobs."

Sally was surprised by the line manager's frankness. "We won't keep Mr Collins longer than necessary, I promise."

He left the room, and Collins made his way around the desk to sit in the manager's chair.

"What's this all about?"

"First of all, we'd like to know why you took off yesterday before our colleagues had a chance to speak with you."

His eyes narrowed, and he picked out a pen from the plastic tidy. "I had an urgent appointment with someone."

"May I ask who?"

His eyes fluttered shut then swiftly opened again. He hitched up a shoulder. "I can't remember."

"You seriously expect us to believe that, Mr Collins?"

"Yes, why? When it's the truth."

Sighing, Sally and Lorne sat on the two plastic chairs in front of him.

"Anyway, it doesn't matter," Sally said. "We're glad to be able to have this chat with you today, instead. I prefer to listen to what a valuable witness has to say for myself, so all is good for me."

"Valuable witness? Am I missing something? You haven't told me what this meeting is about yet."

"Then let me fill you in on that score."

He nodded. "Please do."

"First of all, I think we need to introduce ourselves properly. We're DI Sally Parker and DS Lorne Warner, detectives associated with the Cold Case Team." She paused until the penny dropped. Except there was no real display of emotion from him. "We're investigating a case that led nowhere a couple of years ago. Do you have any idea which case I might be referring to?"

"I might look stupid, Inspector, but I assure you, I'm far from it. You're here about Christian Starr. Go on, tell me I'm wrong."

"No, you're one hundred percent correct. As a matter of procedure, when we revisit an investigation like this, we try and track down all the witnesses, friends and associates of the missing person who were interviewed at the time."

"Why? If they've already been interviewed, why bother with them again?"

"I would have thought that was obvious—in case anything was missed the first time around."

"Such as?"

"You tell me. Can you recall the interview you had with DI Kirkland back in twenty-two?"

"Vividly, thanks."

A smirk appeared on his face that Sally was itching to slap. "Good, in that case, you won't mind going over the information you gave to the SIO one more time."

He blew out a breath. "I'll give it a go. What do you want to know?"

"All of it."

"Is it possible for you to be more specific?"

"Christian was your best friend, wasn't he?"

"Yes."

"Is that still the case today?"

"He'll always be regarded as my best friend, yes."

"Sorry, what I meant was, do you have any interaction with him these days?"

He tutted and frowned. "I have no idea where this line of questioning is going. Care to enlighten me?"

"Putting it simply, since Christian left his family, have you seen him?"

"No."

"I see. Before he went missing, did he ever discuss with you what his intentions were?"

"No. Next?"

"So, you're telling me, as close as you were to him, you being his *best mate*, that you never held a conversation about your private lives?"

"Did I say that? Of course we did. You asked if he told me what his intentions were, and I said no. That's the truth. Christian disappearing like that was as much of a shock to me as it was to Zara and his family. How is she by the way? Moved on yet? Found another fella, has she? Oh no, she can't, doesn't she have to wait seven years before she does that? Isn't that the law?"

"You seem pretty well-informed on such matters, Mr Collins."

"Something I've picked up along the way. They say you learn something new every day, don't they? How is she?"

"Actually, she's not very well at all."

He fidgeted and gulped. "I'm sorry to hear that. What's wrong with her?"

"I'd rather leave it at that, if you don't mind."

"Fair enough. Anything else you want to know, or is that it?"

"You can tell me if you've ever had any contact with Christian since he disappeared."

"No, not in the slightest. He not only drove out of his family's life that night but also mine."

"And that upset you, did it?"

"No. If you must know, it made me angry rather than upset. He had always been like a brother to me. Neither of us had siblings growing up, I think that's what drew us to each other at school."

"Ah, so you were long-term friends then. What age did you start hanging around together?"

"At the beginning of secondary school."

"Just the two of you, or did you belong to a group who hung around together?"

"Nope, just us." He inclined his head. "Anything else you need to know about that?"

"Did you live close to each other?"

"Yes, reasonably close throughout our childhood. We even started Saturday jobs together, working at Halfords."

"Going back to the day he went missing, or just before, did he share with you any concerns he had regarding either his home life or his business?"

"No, nothing at all."

"And you didn't find that strange?"

"Why would I, if I had no idea of what was going on? You're asking these questions as if you're suspicious of me. Why? Just because I was his friend?"

"Sorry if that's the way it's coming across. All we're trying to do is search for answers. It's been two years since he disappeared. I can't believe, if you were that close from a very young age, he upped and left without saying a single word to you about going."

"If you don't believe me, then that's your choice. Only I know what the truth is. What else can I tell you? If you're expecting me to blurt out that I know where he is, then you're way off the mark, Inspector. As I've already stated, Christian taking off like that angered me to the extreme because of how solid our friendship was."

"Okay, setting that aside then, what do you believe happened to him?"

"I haven't got a clue and, right now, I couldn't give a shit. Friends don't do what he did."

"What if something serious happened to him that night and he didn't just disappear?"

"I don't know. I've tried to wrap my head around this more times than I care to remember, and I can't get past the feeling of betrayal that churns me up inside."

"Did Christian ever divulge the fact that he had taken out loans against the house and the business?"

"No, never. I was shocked and appalled when Zara told me the letters hit the doormat a few days later. She asked if I knew. When I told her I didn't, I think she thought I was lying. I wasn't. The whole thing made a farce out of my friendship with Christian. I thought I knew him inside and out, but I was wrong."

"If this behaviour was unlike him, why have you felt the need to come out against him?"

"Have I? All I've told you is that I feel let down by him. If he's still out there, he obviously wants nothing more to do with me. There's not a lot I can do about that. If, on the other hand, something sinister happened to him, then surely, wouldn't we have heard about it by now? I spent months, out there every night, searching for him, as did his family. All of our efforts were in vain. You tell me what we're supposed to make of that."

"And yet you haven't kept in touch with his family. May I ask why?"

"Too damn hard. It wasn't my responsibility to take care of Zara and Mila, it was his. If he ran off because he couldn't hack the pressure of married life and running a business, why should it have been down to me to pick up the pieces?"

"Instead, you decided it would be best to take a clean break from all of them?"

"Correct. What would you have done in the circumstances?"

Sally stared at him, still unsure whether he was revealing the truth or not. "Hard to say. I think you need to live in someone else's shoes for a while before you can make a call of that nature."

"Anyway, I think I've done my best to answer all of your questions, so I need to get back to work now, while I still have a job."

"Is that a possibility?"

"You heard what Tyrell said, nothing is guaranteed these days, not in the manufacturing business, because of Brexit."

"Ah, yes. Well, I want to thank you for speaking with us today. Please, take one of my cards. If you think of anything I should know, will you give me a call?"

"I will. Sorry about yesterday, it really was a genuine emergency that happened at an inconvenient time."

Sally smiled, unconvinced. "These things are sent to try us."

He showed them back to the locker room, and from there they found their way back to the reception area.

"All done?" the receptionist asked.

"Yes, thanks for your help."

Outside, in the cool fresh air, Sally cursed under her breath. "He was a frustrating bastard."

Lorne laughed. "You're telling me. I'm still not convinced he revealed the truth, are you?"

"Not at all. I'm wondering whether we should put him under surveillance. What do you reckon?"

Lorne shook her head. "Just because the conversation you had with him was dubious, you're going to need to have more to go on than that when funds are tight, Sal."

"You're right. Let's face it, this investigation is leading us nowhere fast."

"Don't lose hope. Another couple of hours and all that could turn upside down."

"Fancy a coffee and a cake somewhere?"

"I'll have a coffee. I'm trying to cut out the sweet things these days."

Sally raised an eyebrow and laughed. "And how long do you foresee that lasting? Given what we ate at the café."

"I'm hopeful. Let's leave it at that, for now."

FEELING REPLETE, after having a coffee and a cheeky iced bun in Sally's case, they headed back to the station where Sally prepared for the conference. It had been a few years since she'd sat on the stage and asked the public for their help with a case, and the butterflies were fluttering wildly in her gut, apparently with nowhere to go.

"Are you all right?" Georgia leaned in to ask.

"I guess I'll reveal all afterwards. I have a lump the size of a melon lodged in my throat that I'm struggling to shift."

Georgia rubbed Sally's forearm. "It'll be a breeze. Just be yourself, and no one will notice how worried you are."

"Great pep talk, it's a pity I don't believe you. I'm fine, don't worry about me. It's what's at stake that is concerning me."

"I figured that. You're going to nail it. That's all the seats filled now, we're good to go. I'll introduce you, and then it's over to you."

"Thanks, I think."

Sally tried to swallow down the lump wedged in her throat, but it refused to budge. She coughed and then began the conference, slotting into her rhythm like an old pro. A few of the more important journalists asked valid questions about how the initial investigation had failed, and Sally did her best to answer every point they raised without stumbling. Finally, she ended the conference, looking down the lens of the TV camera, pleading for Christian himself to come forward for the sake of his daughter.

The journalists filed out of the room, and Georgia accompanied Sally up the stairs to her office.

"You were brilliant back there."

"I wouldn't say that. Now all we have to do is sit back and wait for all the calls to come in."

"Let me know how it goes, Sally. Give me a shout if I can do anything else to help."

"Organising the conference with less than a day's notice is going above and beyond in my opinion. Speak soon." She waved farewell and joined her team.

The afternoon dragged by, the team on tenterhooks, waiting for the phones to ring. They remained silent, much to Sally's annoyance and regret.

THE FOLLOWING DAY, Sally received a frantic call from the desk sergeant.

"Sorry to disturb you, ma'am, I thought you should know straight away."

"What's that, Pat?"

"I've had a call from the hospital. The staff found a man in Zara Starr's room. He ran off before security could apprehend him."

"Jesus, do we know who it was? What he wanted? Did he harm her?"

"Sorry, that's all the information I have. Just passing it on, ma'am."

"Thanks for letting me know. Will you put an officer on duty outside her room ASAP?"

"Consider it done."

"Thanks, Pat." Sally hung up and slammed the phone back in its cradle. "Lorne," she shouted.

Lorne instantly appeared in the doorway. "You yelled. Hey, what's wrong? I know that look, you're troubled about something. Have you had a call? Someone come forward with some information?"

"No, nothing like that. Pat rang, told me that a man was found in Zara's hospital room this morning."

"What the...? Was she hurt?"

"The information was sketchy. I think we need to get over there."

Lorne pulled a face. "Was the man captured?"

"No, he ran off. Why?"

"Maybe it would be a wasted trip for us."

"What would you do?"

"Not doubt myself. Do what you need to do, Sally."

"Christ, I thought Jack was frustrating to work alongside. What about CCTV footage? That's going to be the key here, isn't it?"

"Possibly. What if it's Christian?"

"The thought had crossed my mind. Maybe he saw the conference. I mentioned Zara was ill in Norwich hospital. Was that a major mistake on my part?"

"I don't think so. Do we know if his visit was to cause mischief?"

"I haven't got a clue. Why would he go and see her? I wonder if he paid Mila a visit."

"We're presuming it's him, hard not to. But I thought he would have contacted you directly. Oh, I don't know, I'm not getting a good feeling about this."

Sally tipped her head back and exhaled. "Neither am I. I'm making the call. Get your coat, we'll shoot over to the hospital."

. . .

The atmosphere in the car was strained.

"If it's him, do you think his conscience has pricked him into action?" Lorne asked.

"Your guess is as good as mine. None of this is panning out the way I imagined it would."

"We're still in the dark, and the tunnel appears to be getting darker instead of lighter."

"It sure does."

Sally parked close to the main entrance, and they dashed through the corridor to Zara's room.

"Hi, how are you doing?" Sally asked Zara who was sitting up in bed, wringing her hands.

She stared at them and whispered, "I think it was him."

"Are you sure?"

"No, not entirely. I'm so confused. He caught me off-guard."

Sally tried to reassure her with a smile. "You're safe. We've put an officer outside your door. He'll remain there for however long you need him."

"Thank God," Zara muttered, her gaze fixed on the door.

"Did he say anything to you, Zara?"

"No. I woke up and found him by my bed, staring at me. I wasn't sure how to react, whether I should be scared of him or grateful that he had come forward, but then he was gone again. Did he get in touch with you, after the appeal went out?"

"No, this is the first sighting we've received of him. He must have been out there, possibly living close by, all this time."

"How do we know that? When the appeal went out, was that to the immediate area?"

"No, it went nationally. His showing up has reinforced the fact that he still cares and all is not lost."

Zara frowned and shook her head. "Does it? Why didn't

he speak to me instead of scaring the crap out of me? I have so many questions I want to ask him. Why did he run off like that and not bother hanging around? Why? Why? Why?" The tears of frustration flowed and dripped onto her cheeks.

Sally sat on the bed beside her and placed a hand over hers. "The fact that he showed up has reinforced that all is not lost. Let's bear that in mind and think of the positives."

"How can you say that? What if he came here to hurt me?"

"Had that been the case, then I think he would have found a way of doing it, don't you?"

"I'm not so sure. What happens now? How was he allowed to get away? Is he likely to return with a copper standing guard outside?"

"They're all valid questions that, at present, I'm unable to answer. We're going to find out what camera footage is available. If we get a clear image of the person, I'll drop by and see if you can make a formal identification."

"And if I can't?"

"I'm not even considering that outcome, not yet. It's far too early to be contemplating the negatives. Has the doctor given you anything to calm you down?"

"No, I refused to take anything. I'm worried about Mila. I know she's safe, it was the first thing I asked, but what if he's determined to get to us? To hurt either one of us?"

Sally raised her hands. "It's all speculation at this stage. I believe if his intentions were to hurt you, he would have done it by now, when the opportunity presented itself."

"So, you think he came back to help? Is about to do the right thing for his daughter?"

"We won't know for sure unless he makes contact with us. Seeing how vulnerable you are might prick his conscience even more. I think we're going to need to give him time, time to do the right thing, for all of you."

"I hope you're right, Inspector, because the last time I looked, time was running out fast for my daughter."

Sally stood, her hand still clinging to Zara's. "I know. All I ask is that you don't give up on me." She squeezed Zara's hand then released it gently.

"I'm trying, believe me, but it's not going to be easy, not when we don't know what his intentions are or how he's going to react when you eventually find him."

"I know. Try to get some rest now. We'll call back once we've had a word with security."

Zara sighed, and her eyes flickered shut.

Sally and Lorne left the room. The officer in the hallway gave them a hesitant smile.

"Do not leave this room," Sally said. "I'm going to have a word with the security guard. You can work things out between you if you need to take a toilet break."

"Yes, ma'am."

They dashed back down the hallway to the small reception desk at the end.

"Sorry to interrupt," Sally said. "I'm looking for the security room, if you have such a thing?"

"Mick is wandering around here somewhere. Hang on, I'll contact him via the radio, he's a nightmare for ignoring his mobile while on duty." She left her desk and picked up a small radio sitting on the shelf behind her. "Mick, it's Rochelle, can you drop by and see me?"

"On my way."

Heavy footsteps sounded moments later, and the man appeared. "Hi, you wanted to see me?"

Rochelle gestured towards Sally and Lorne. "These ladies do."

Sally produced her ID. "Do you have any footage we can go through?"

"Ah, yes. I should have thought about that myself. Sorry, I got distracted by another task."

"Can we do it now? Time is of the essence."

He turned on his heel, and they had to jog to keep up with his long strides. Once they were inside his tiny office, he fiddled with the machine, and they all watched the images spring to life on the screen.

"Is that him?" Lorne asked.

At the bottom, Sally could make out a man in dark clothing. He shielded his face as he made his way up the corridor.

"Probably. Let me try and get a better view of him from a different angle."

"That's it. Can you zoom in?" Sally asked, her heart racing. *Please, please let it be him. It would be wonderful if he'd had a twinge of conscience and put his daughter first.* In her mind, Sally conjured up the photo they had of Christian on the original file and nodded. "There's no doubt, I believe it's him. What about you, Lorne?"

"I absolutely agree. Can you tell us which way he went? Whether he visited his daughter on the other side of the hospital?"

"Ah, that's going to take me a while to trawl through the footage. As you can see, I only have very limited equipment to hand. I'm sounding like a broken record, keep telling them it all needs updating, but all they give me is the same lame excuses as to why they don't have the funds to chuck our way. That's all well and good until something like this happens."

"If you can do your best for us? We're going to sprint over the other side, check on Zara's daughter while we're here."

"Leave it with me. Is this guy dangerous?"

"We're not sure. I don't think so. The truth is he's been missing for two years, and we don't have a clue where he's been hiding out or what he's been up to."

"But he's done the right thing, coming forward for his daughter, right?"

"Apparently not, because he's on the run," Sally felt the need to correct him.

"Ah, yes. Maybe if I hadn't shouted and chased after him... sorry about that."

"Nonsense, you were doing what you thought was right. We'll call back and see you soon."

He nodded and began jabbing at the buttons as they left the room.

They were both out of breath by the time they reached Mila's room.

"Let's take a second or two to recover. The last thing we want is to show up flustered, it's not a good look." Sally placed her hands on her hips and sucked in a lungful of steadying breaths.

"I'm good to go," Lorne stated.

"Give me a second. Shows how unfit I am."

Lorne chuckled. "It would appear that mucking out dog kennels in the evening is beneficial after all."

"A definite plus. Okay, I'm back." Sally knocked on the door and entered the room to find Amy Walters sitting in the chair next to Mila, holding her hand. In her lap, there was a ball of wool with knitting needles speared through it.

"How are you?" Sally whispered. She could tell by the black surrounding her eyes that Amy hadn't had much sleep since she'd been forced to stay at the hospital.

"I'm doing okay. Shall we talk outside? Mila has only just dropped off to sleep."

They crept out of the room, and Amy closed the door gently behind her. "Leslie has gone to buy us some lunch or brunch, I forget which it is. Neither of us has left the hospital since we arrived."

"That's admirable of you both, but you still need your rest."

"I can rest when I'm dead. Are you here to share the news you've received from the appeal?"

Chewing the inside of her mouth, Sally wondered if she should share Christian's reappearance with Amy or not. A noise sounded behind her, and Leslie came around the corner carrying two paper cups and a couple of sandwiches.

"Oh, you're back. Hopefully with good news for us," Leslie said. He handed one lot of food and drink to his wife. "Well?" His eyes narrowed. "Wait, has something happened?"

"I'm sorry, yes, it has. We received a call, informing us that a man was found in Zara's room earlier. We rushed to get here."

Amy placed her sandwich and drink on the chair beside her then clutched her husband's hand. "Oh no, was she harmed?"

"No, she's a little shaken up, but other than that, she appears to be fine. We've put an officer outside her room, just to ensure she remains safe."

"And what about Mila?" Leslie demanded.

"Yes, we'll do the same for Mila. We're waiting for another officer to arrive. Did you see anyone hanging around earlier?"

"No, we've been in there with Mila all morning, all night, since she came in. We're shattered, but it doesn't matter to us," Leslie replied. "Has he come forward to offer Mila his kidney?"

"Hard to say what's going on in his head at this time."

"Where is he now?" Amy asked. She picked up her coffee and removed the top to take a sip.

"He ran off, escaped the security guard," Sally confirmed. "We're going to do our best to find him."

Lorne stepped away from them and withdrew her phone from her pocket. Sally's focus remained with Mila's grandparents.

"Why doesn't he just front up? Show himself? What has he got to lose?" Leslie shook his head. "It's not like he's broken the law, has he?"

"Actually, he has. He possibly forged your daughter's signature on the loans he took out."

"Sorry, I was forgetting that aspect. All I'm concerned about is Mila's and Zara's health issues. What a man, eh? Jesus, he should be the one sitting here with his daughter, holding her hand while she sleeps. Well, if he doesn't come forward and get tested within the next day or so, that lass will be permanently asleep."

"Leslie, don't be so callous. We need to cling to the hope that he'll do the right thing."

"I fear you're going to be waiting a long time, dear. He's had two years to do the right thing and come out of the woodwork. He's failed to do it, and now look what state his wife and daughter are in. What a bloody sorry excuse for a man he is."

"We don't know the reasons behind his absence," Sally added. "I'm not making excuses for him, far from it, but until we can find him and ask him what's going on, I think we should refrain from being too harsh with our criticism." She struggled to believe the words had tumbled out of her mouth.

Leslie's face turned the colour of hot coals. "Perhaps if you feel that way, Inspector, maybe you're not the right person to be working on this case."

Amy slapped her husband's chest. "Don't be so rude,

Leslie. The inspector has shown us nothing but kindness so far. I'm more than happy to keep dealing with her."

"Thank you, Amy. We're doing our best with the evidence we have to hand, Mr Walters."

He grumbled something incoherent and turned his back on Sally. She glanced sideways, noted that Lorne was frowning and excused herself.

"What's wrong?"

Lorne kept her voice low. "Sorry, I thought I would step in and organise a sweep of the area while you spoke to the Walters."

"I thought you might. Thanks for having my back, Lorne."

"There's more. While I was on the phone to Pat, he received a call from Zara's neighbour."

"What? Shit, I'm not going to like this, am I?"

"Nope. She was pottering around in the garden and heard someone in Zara's back garden. She went upstairs to get a better view. The door was open, but there was no one around."

"Shit. Were they inside the house or had they run off? Christ, it has to be him, what's he up to? How did he know where she lived?"

Lorne shrugged. "Perhaps he's known all along."

"Fuck, that's a possibility?"

"We won't know until we find him and bring him in for questioning. Anyway, I called the patrols off in the end. It would be pointless them showing up to search the hospital grounds if he's already been seen back there."

"He got back there quickly, which means he has access to a vehicle."

Lorne waved her hand in front of her. "That's not difficult these days."

"What does he want? Why go to the house, knowing that his wife and daughter are both seriously ill in hospital?"

"Desperation? I don't really know."

"Get forensics over there, let's make sure it's him. Put another officer outside the house. It'll act as a deterrent, if nothing else."

Lorne stepped away to relay the instructions.

"What's going on?" Leslie ordered.

"Nothing for you to be concerned about."

"Why don't I believe you?" he challenged.

"Leslie, stop it," Amy shouted. "You coming down heavily on the inspector like this isn't doing anyone any good."

He slumped into the chair beside him and then bounced back to his feet again and entered his granddaughter's room, closing the door firmly behind him.

"I'm sorry, you'll have to forgive him, Inspector. I can assure you, he's only speaking for himself."

"I'm glad to hear it, Amy. We truly are doing our best. We're up against it because Christian has been elusive for the past two years. He's come back into the limelight for a reason. Let's hope it's the right one."

"To save his daughter? We can only hope. She's fading fast. Surely, he should know that would be the case, after the appeal you put out."

"You'd think so. We'll have to wait and see," Sally replied, deflated.

"Where do we go from here? Is he liable to return to the hospital? What if he changes his mind and that's the last anyone sees of him?" Amy covered her face with her hands. "No, no, I shouldn't have said that. Now I'm going to be sat in there, thinking the worst. My poor Mila, she doesn't deserve this. Why won't her father come forward if he has nothing to hide?"

"I'm hopeful. If he's attempted to make contact with Zara once, there's every chance he'll do it again." Sensing the conversation was about to continue going over old ground,

Sally decided to end it. "Okay, there's little else we can do here. We'll go back, check how Zara is before we hit the road again. Will you be okay?"

"I think so. Good luck finding him. You didn't tell us if the appeal had been a success or not. Did you receive any calls?"

"A few, but they turned out to be false leads. This is the closest we've come to finding him, we won't give up."

Sally and Lorne returned to pay Zara a visit. She appeared to be more settled now and grateful there was an officer stationed outside.

"He will be here all the time, won't he?"

"You have my word. We dropped by to tell you Mila is doing okay, despite this little blip."

"Thank you, I was worried about her. What will you do now?"

"We're going to make sure every officer in the area is on full alert until we find him." Sally had no intention of telling Zara that Christian may have already broken into her house.

"I'm not a religious person, Inspector, but I will be saying several prayers tonight."

Sally smiled, and they left the room. She reinforced the magnitude of the situation to the officer on guard.

"You can rely on me, ma'am."

"Good. Here's my direct number, don't hesitate to use it. Keep vigilant at all times."

The officer took the card and tucked it into his top pocket. "I'll be sure to contact you, ma'am. I'll guard her with my life."

"Good. I'll be checking in regularly until we've managed to locate her husband." Her mobile rang. She excused herself and answered it, but not before she took a couple of steps up the corridor towards the entrance. "DI Sally Parker, how may I help?"

"It's Pat, ma'am. Sorry to interrupt, I have more news that I thought you should know straight away."

Sally rolled her eyes at Lorne. "Go on, surprise me."

"We've had a call from Julie Granger. I believe you know her, ma'am."

"That's correct. She's Zara Starr's sister. Is there something wrong?"

"She called the station to report a break-in at her home."

"Sod it, not again. Was she there when it happened?"

"No, she and her husband were both at work at the time. She decided to pop back to the house at lunchtime and discovered the back door was open and the place had been ransacked."

"We're on our way back from Norwich now. We'll call in to see her en route. Is her husband with her, or is she alone?"

"Her husband is there with her. He's arranged for a locksmith to do the necessary at the house."

"And is Julie okay?"

"A little shaken up." The phone rang in the background. "Sorry, I'm by myself here. Can you hold the line?"

"Call me back. We'll make our way to the car and get on the road."

En route, Sally explained to Lorne what had happened at Julie's.

"I wonder what he's after," Lorne said.

Sally started the engine and pulled out of the car park. "Hard to know, isn't it?" Her phone rang, and this time she put it on speaker. "Pat, anything for us?"

"Yes, another interesting phone call has just come my way, ma'am."

"We're listening. Is this from the appeal?"

"It is. A young woman, Nancy Chan called to say that she had seen Christian Starr, or a man who very much looked like him, in her corner shop the other day."

"The other day? And she remembered him because?"

"She couldn't put her finger on why he struck her as strange, just that he did."

"Can you get someone from my team around there to take a statement? I think we should prioritise paying Julie a visit."

"I'll get on it now. Good luck."

Sally ended the call and took a swipe at the steering wheel. "Why? Why keep hidden for two years and suddenly resurface?"

"Obviously he's in turmoil about what is going on with his daughter, not so much what's happening with Zara, although he has paid her a visit."

"Yeah, you're right. But I've got a feeling this is about so much more than *just* that his wife and child are both in hospital."

"We can speculate until the cows come home, but the truth is, we don't know the man or how his mind works, and until we catch up with him, we're as much in the dark as he wants us to be."

## CHAPTER 8

A man was changing the locks on the front door when they arrived at the house.

"Is Mrs Granger in?" Sally asked.

He stood to one side, allowing them to enter. "They're both inside."

"Thanks." Sally pushed the door open and called out, "Julie, are you here?"

A man with a neatly trimmed goatee, wearing gym clothes, appeared in the hallway. "Who are you?"

Sally and Lorne produced their warrant cards.

"DI Sally Parker and DS Lorne Warner. Is Julie around?"

"In here. Why has this been allowed to happen?" he demanded, his angry glare boring into Sally the closer she got to him.

"Why don't we sit down and have a chat? You can tell us how things unfolded."

"More time wasted when you should be out there, searching for the bastard," he ranted.

Julie was sitting in the lounge, her hands linked together.

"Oh, you're here. I don't profess to know what's going on, but I wish you would make it stop."

Sally and Lorne sat on the sofa opposite.

"Why don't you run through what happened?" Sally asked.

"I got home from work—I returned at lunchtime because I had forgotten to pick up some important paperwork I needed for a lesson this afternoon. I don't usually check the back door, but the house was colder than normal and I went to see if the boiler was okay. That's when I saw the door was open and that a pane of glass had been broken."

"Did you see anyone?"

"No. I ran through the house, grabbed my handbag and phone and legged it out to the car. After locking myself in, I rang Martin right away. He told me to ring the police. Sorry, I mislaid your card, otherwise I would have called you directly. I decided to swap my bag over this morning."

"That's okay, the desk sergeant tends to have a general idea of what cases we're working on. He rang me while we were at the hospital."

She gasped and frowned. "Why were you there? No, don't tell me… is it Mila? Has she suffered a setback?"

"No. We were alerted to the fact that Zara discovered a strange man in her room earlier."

"Shit! Did he harm her?" She glanced up and reached out a hand to her husband.

Martin sat on the arm of the chair.

"No, he startled her."

"Who was it? Does she know?" Martin asked.

"She believes it was Christian and CCTV footage confirms it."

"Jesus. After all this time? But this is good news, isn't it? Him turning up at the hospital? Did he visit his daughter? Is he going to help out? Give up his kidney to save her?"

Sally raised a hand. "We need to keep an eye on our expectations. He ran off before Zara could get anything out of him. Since then, we've had reports that Zara's house was broken into and received a call from yourselves, saying the same. Can you think of any reason why, if the incidences were down to Christian? What he might have been after?"

Martin tutted. "You tell us. You're the bloody coppers, not us."

"In our opinion, he must have come back for something. To be in hiding for two years and to suddenly break his cover, it doesn't ring true that this has anything to do with what's going on with Mila. So, any suggestions you might have will help us immensely."

"Because he's a twisted fucker who enjoys toying with his family. Zara and Mila have struggled to make ends meet since the day he walked out on them. He left them riddled with debts. Now he's returned, while they're both incapacitated. Why? To cause both of them yet more angst?"

"We're none the wiser," Sally replied.

"What I want to know is what you're doing about it," Martin said. He flung an arm around his wife's shoulder and pulled her close.

"Can you do anything?" Julie asked.

"We're trying. We have a few leads we're chasing up at the moment, and there are several patrol cars circulating the area on the lookout for him."

"Let's face it, you haven't got a clue where he is, have you?" Martin sneered.

"Not right at this second. As the information hits us, we're doing what we can to locate him."

"It's simply not good enough," Martin insisted. "How has this man been allowed to wander around the area when he's been on the missing list for a couple of years? Do you know where he's living?"

"No. We're still receiving calls from the general public with possible sightings. As you can imagine, each call takes a while to investigate."

"In the meantime, he's still free and walking the streets, being allowed to cause mayhem to all of us connected to this family. How is that possible? What do you intend to do to rectify the situation, Inspector?"

"Everything that is necessary. I'm glad you're taking the precaution of changing the locks, that's the first thing I would have suggested."

"It's a waste of time in my opinion, but it'll make Julie feel better. He broke a window to get in, he didn't use a key or mess around with the locks."

Julie shot him a challenging look. "I know that, I'm not stupid. It's the security and peace of mind I need, not you putting me down, Martin. So back off."

He withdrew his arm from her shoulder and stood. "I'll leave you ladies to it. I sense as a man, I'm in the way around here."

"Don't be so ridiculous," Julie called after him before the door slammed shut. "Excuse him, he hates feeling out of control of a situation. He wasn't happy that I demanded he should be here when the locksmith arrived either. Tough shit, I'm not going to deal with all this crap myself."

"Sorry you've been subjected to this, Julie. Is there anything you can tell us that you believe will point us in the right direction?"

"No, nothing. I've gone over it a thousand times already. We weren't close with my sister and her husband. So, Christian coming here is a mystery that I'm unable to get my head around." Tears trickled.

Sally plucked a tissue from the box beside her and handed it to Julie. "Here, okay. Have you had a chance to look around yet? To see if there is anything missing?"

"No, the main items are still here, the TV et cetera. I had my laptop at work with me."

"What about Martin? Has he mentioned anything is missing?"

"No, nothing at all. Which is a puzzle in itself, isn't it? Why, if it's Christian, would he break into our house and not take anything?"

"Something we'll need to ask him when we eventually find him."

"Are Zara and Mila okay? I've been meaning to set some time aside to go and visit them, but my job is pretty full-on most days."

"Yes, they're both doing as well as expected. I'm sure Zara would be happy to see you, when you can spare the time to travel to the hospital."

"That's just it, it's quite a trek out there, just to sit awkwardly with her. Are my parents still there?"

"Yes, they're sitting next to Mila, I suspect praying for a miracle."

"Shit, why can't Christian do the right thing for once and come forward? Why is he intent on causing all this aggro? None of it is making any sense to me. Unless that's his intention… to keep us all on our toes before he makes his next move."

"Perhaps. Try not to worry too much. We've got all the bases covered. There are officers standing guard outside Zara's and Mila's rooms. The second he's spotted, he'll be arrested."

"I'm glad to see that you're taking it seriously. What about us?"

Sally inclined her head. "Sorry? What about you?"

"Are you going to offer us protection?"

"We don't have the manpower to protect all the family. All

I can do is ensure a patrol car drives past periodically day and night, if that will help?"

Julie shook her head. "I can't believe this. He breaks in here, and you're not prepared to go the extra mile for us? What about putting us up somewhere in a safe house?"

"There's a problem with that—he hasn't actually made any threats towards you. Yes, he might have broken in, if it was him. You've said yourself that you don't know who it was. The other issue we have is that witness protection isn't set up for incidents of this nature. They're in place for people whose lives have been threatened."

Julie's head sank, and she dabbed at her eyes with the tissue. "So, what you're effectively telling us is that we're on our own? That we have to fend for ourselves, if he shows up here wielding a knife at my throat?"

Sally shrugged. "I wish there was more we could do to help."

"You can get out there and arrest him, get him off the streets, because he's obviously a threat to society. How do we know what his mental state is? We don't, and yet you're willing to pooh-pooh my concerns as if they don't mean a thing. I thought it was the job of the police to protect the general public."

"It is, and we're doing that with your sister and her daughter. If you're that worried about him coming to the house, maybe it would be better if you stayed elsewhere for a few days."

"Where? Why should I give up my security and comfort?"

"What about Martin's parents? Can you stay with them?"

"No, we fell out with them years ago."

"A close friend might be willing to help you out."

"Ha, I would feel bad if anything happened to them while we were staying at their house."

"Then I'm sorry, I've run out of ideas."

"Sounds about right for a copper in these parts to say," she snapped back.

Sally stared at her for a few seconds and then rose to her feet. "We need to get on with our day now. I'm glad you're safe. My only advice would be that you remain vigilant at all times."

"Oh, don't worry, I will. Let's hope you catch the bastard soon."

Julie stayed where she was, and Sally and Lorne left the room. Sally groaned internally the second she saw the pissed-off expression on Martin's face in the hallway.

"We'll be in touch if we uncover anything."

"What? Is that it? A two-minute visit and then you're out of here?"

"There's little we can do once the perpetrator has left the scene. Have Forensics been in touch?"

"Yes, they said they were on their way. That was twenty minutes ago. Seems to me we're the only ones around here who are taking this seriously."

"That's not the case at all, Mr Granger."

"Whatever." He stood aside.

Sally and Lorne squeezed through the front door once the locksmith had also taken a step back.

"I'm getting ticked off with this family having a go at me."

"Us," Lorne corrected.

They entered the car under the watchful eye of Martin Granger.

"I repeat, there's got to be more to this than meets the eye," Sally said.

"I'm inclined to agree with you, but what?"

"I've run out of ideas. Why would he break in, hit both of their houses? He must be searching for something. What? And why has it taken him two years to come looking for it?"

"Pass. What's concerning me is that he's intent on

searching for something and yet his daughter has a life-threatening condition. That should be his priority, shouldn't it?"

THEY HAD REACHED the halfway point on their journey back to the station when Sally's phone rang.

"I'm getting twitchy about answering it. Can you get it for me? Put it on speaker."

"Don't allow it to get to you. Your phone rings dozens of times a day, and you never usually bat an eyelid."

"Yes, Mum."

"DI Sally Parker's phone," Lorne answered.

"Sorry to trouble you yet again, ladies, but I think it would be negligent of me not to keep you up to date on things as they occur."

"Stop waffling and get on with it, Pat," Sally admonished light-heartedly.

"I wasn't aware that I was. Okay, brace yourselves for this one."

Sally and Lorne both gestured with their hands for him to hurry.

"We're teetering on the edge of our seats with anticipation," Sally teased.

"Then I'll begin. Around thirty minutes ago we received a call from a member of the public who had witnessed a car accident. The two men involved got out of their vehicles and squared up to each other. Then they started knocking seven bells out of each other. All the witnesses were female, so the caller said, and none of them really wanted to get involved."

"Fair enough. Did a patrol vehicle show up?"

"Yes, but it was too late."

"Too late? Come on, Pat, this isn't like you. Get to the point and quickly."

"One of the men thrashed the living daylights out of the other man, knocked him unconscious and threw him into his own vehicle. The perpetrator chose to leave his car at the scene, if that makes sense."

"It does, but why? Have you run the plates?"

"On the car that was left behind at the scene, yes. It was stolen from Attleborough last night, sometime after ten."

"What about the plate on the car that got away?" Sally asked. She pulled into a lay-by.

"Here's the thing, the witness only caught half the number, but it was the important part. I ran it through the system and discovered that the car belongs to a Perry Walters."

Sally thumped the steering wheel. "Shit. And have you had a chance to trace the vehicle?"

"Not yet. I'm alone on reception, and it's been a busy morning already, as you know."

"Too right. Okay, will you pass the details of the incident over to my team? Ask them to search the local cameras. Let's see if we can find out in which direction the car went."

"I'll arrange that now, ma'am."

Lorne punched the 'End Call' button on Sally's mobile. "It was only a matter of time before he made his move."

Sally considered her partner's suggestion and then started the engine again. "What's your game, mister?"

TEN MINUTES LATER, they flew through the main entrance and up the stairs to the office.

"Anything yet?" Sally asked. She tore off her jacket and hung it on the nearby coat stand.

"I've got the footage lined up for you to see," Jordan said.

Sally and Lorne stood behind him and watched the images play out on the screen.

"Ouch, he wasn't holding back, was he?" Sally observed. She winced a couple of times at the ferocity of the strikes.

"Seems to be determined to bring him down and get on with things," Lorne said. "Have you managed to locate the vehicle after it left the area?"

"Still trying to do that. I've only had the footage for about ten minutes," Jordan replied.

"Hang on, is this the same area where the other witness said she thinks she saw Christian in the shop?"

"Yes, that's right. Set in the middle of the family's homes."

"Very interesting. Okay, keep going with this, Jordan. Let's see what this man has in his locker." Sally grabbed a coffee and brought the whiteboard up to date.

"What are you thinking?" Lorne perched her backside on the desk beside her.

"That we're still scrabbling around for clues. He's upped the ante by kidnapping Perry. The reason behind the abduction is still mystifying, though, and it shouldn't be, not at this stage."

"It's perplexing to say the least. Maybe everything will start to fall into place now."

"Maybe. There's still the issue of Christian not coming forward for his own daughter. What's that bloody about? All it's doing is portraying him as a heartless bastard who cares fuck all about anyone but himself."

"Perhaps that's what he wants us to believe," Lorne suggested.

"One break, that's all we need."

Jordan joined them. "I think I might have something for you, boss. I followed the car's route as far as I could, and it led to the docks at King's Lynn."

"Well, that's hopeful. Anybody here know that area?"

"Not really," Jordan replied.

The rest of the team responded the same.

"Right, we're going to need to flood the area with patrol cars. Hit the docks before he gets away. What time was the last sighting of his vehicle?"

"At one-thirty-three."

Sally glanced at her watch—just over an hour. "There's a chance we could be too late. Why head for the dock?"

"Could be a number of reasons. What about using it as a storage centre? Or he might have jumped on board a boat that was due to leave the dock," Lorne suggested.

"Let's get on the road and see for ourselves. Jordan and Stuart, you come with us. Joanna, you stay here and man the phones, if you will?"

"Do you want me to contact the dock, boss?" Joanna asked. "Try and get ahead of the game, organise the CCTV footage for when you get there?"

"Good idea. We'll leave that with you and get on the road."

SALLY AND JORDAN parked their respective cars close to the main office, and the four of them entered the building. Joanna had rung ahead to tell the manager, Mr Pitts, to expect them. He was waiting in his office but joined them as soon as they arrived in the reception area. After introducing himself, he showed them through to a room where the security cameras were set up.

"I've got a few things lined up for you. It brightened my day to be able to help the police. Love a bit of intrigue to break up the monotony around here."

"We can't thank you enough for acting so promptly. It's important that we find these men ASAP. The life of one of them could be in imminent danger."

"This is the car pulling into the yard."

He pointed out the vehicle, and Sally turned to Jordan to corroborate it was the right one.

"That's it."

"Great. Can you fast forward, show us what happened next?"

Pitts hit a couple of buttons, and they watched the car drive to the end of the dock. There, the driver removed the other man from the car. He was awake but seemed very dazed. The two men then walked out of sight.

"Where does that lead?" Sally asked.

"To the storage containers. Most of the ones in that area are there permanently, and those on the other side are the ones we load onto the ships."

Keeping her attention on the screen, Sally asked. "Do you have keys to all the containers?"

"No, the upkeep is the responsibility of the person who hires the containers."

"Can you supply us with a list?"

"I can. Most of them are owned by businesses."

"Regular customers?"

"Yes, mostly. The odd free one comes up now and again."

"Any cameras around that side of the dock?"

"A few. The main cameras are in the high traffic areas, such as around here," Pitts replied.

"It's as if he knows it and has deliberately headed off in that direction. Can you try and pick him up on the other camera?"

Pitts nodded and messed around with the equipment again, this time locating the other camera.

"Jordan, while we're waiting, why don't you and Stuart take a shufty around there? Specifically search for spaces large enough to hide a fully grown man."

The two men left the office.

"Was the car still outside?" Sally asked Lorne.

"Yes, I think so."

"The patrols should be here soon. Then we can carry out a thorough search. Did he seem panicked to you or in total control of the situation?"

"Hard to tell from that distance. He appeared to know where he was going, though, as if he was aware of the area, or maybe he knows someone who works here and was following their instructions to the letter."

"Possibly. Mr Pitts, after you've sorted this out for us, is it possible for you to supply us with a list of your employees?"

"Oh, I see. You believe he has an accomplice? A member of my staff helping him?"

"It's speculation at best, but why else would he come here if he doesn't know how the docks work?"

"I put a lot of trust in my staff, Inspector, I'd be shocked if anyone was assisting him. The docks can be a very dangerous place for people who are untrained."

"I can believe it."

The screen came to life again. "This is what the next camera picked up. I'll leave you to it and sort the other matter out for you."

"Thanks, it's appreciated."

He left the room.

Sally shuffled forward to get a closer look.

"Why here?" Lorne asked.

"I haven't got the foggiest, not unless he's about to ship Perry off somewhere, but where?"

"We need to see the shipping manifest when Pitts returns."

"If it will help. My gut feeling is that he intends to keep Perry here—don't ask me why, none of this is making any sense, so I wouldn't be able to answer. The only certainty we have right now is that we need to capture Christian and find Perry before it's too late."

"I agree. What on earth is going on in Christian's head, kidnapping Perry, especially when his priority should lie with Mila?"

"That's the toughest part about this, the fact that he appears keen to let his daughter down, die, if necessary, because that's what it amounts to, isn't it? How can he sleep at night?"

"And where has he been for the past two years? Living under a pseudonym? What if he's worked here in the past but changed his name? How are we going to tell if we check a list of the employees? We're so far in the dark on this one, scoffing a hundredweight of carrots isn't going to help us see clearly."

Sally grinned. "Even if I loved carrots, I'd still draw the line at eating more than a handful."

She faced the screen again as the two men rounded the corner and came into view. Perry stumbled once or twice, but a few jabs to the stomach from Christian, and Perry was back on his feet and showing willing again.

"Hang on, is that someone else… there, at the bottom?" Lorne pointed to the corner of the screen. The light wasn't good in that area, and it was difficult to make out if the person was waiting for them or not.

The anticipation escalated the closer the two men got to the third man.

"Yes, looks like he has an accomplice here," Lorne said.

Mr Pitts came back into the office. He passed Sally a sheet of paper with around twenty names on it.

She briefly cast her eyes over the list, but nothing jumped out at her. "What do you think, Lorne?"

Sally passed the sheet to Lorne who scan-read it and shook her head.

"None the wiser, sorry," Lorne said.

"It was worth a shot. Mr Pitts, can I draw your attention

to the screen? The two men appear to have met up with this man. Any idea who that is?"

He peered closer but shook his head. "It doesn't look like anyone I know, but the distance isn't doing us any favours, is it?"

"That's true, it's very hard to tell. Let's see where they go from here." Gravel crunched outside the window, and Sally peeked out to find four patrol cars parked in front of the main office. "Our colleagues are here. They'll be needing instructions. Can we pause this for a moment while I deal with them?"

Pitts hit the button, and the screen froze.

Sally raced outside and brought the officers up to date on what they had witnessed on the screen. "This only happened within the last hour. The victim's car is still parked at the bottom there. That's not to say the perpetrator hasn't already got his hands on another vehicle. He seems to have a penchant for stealing cars as far as we can tell. Note down my number. If you see anything suspicious, ring me straight away. Be vigilant and cautious. The dock can be a dangerous area to survey, just be aware of that at all times. Off you go, and if you see Jordan and Stuart from my team, send them back. Thanks."

The officers tore across the car park in the direction of the last possible sighting of the two men.

Despondent, Sally returned to the office. "That's the area flooded. It's either sink or swim for us now."

"Do you want me to press Play again, see if there's anything else that comes up?" Pitts asked.

"If you would. The area is getting darker down there, isn't it? So, this leads to the containers, does it?"

"Yes, that's right, the permanent ones."

. . .

THE HUNT for the men went on for the next hour. Sally paced Pitts' office, the frustration mounting to a new crescendo until she received the call she'd been waiting for.

"Ma'am, we've found him."

"Thank God, is he alive? Where is he?"

"Down at the third dock. I've rung for an ambulance. In my experience it's touch and go."

"I'll come down." Sally ended the call. "He's been found at the third dock. Is there a shortcut we can take?"

"I'll take you myself in the buggy," Mr Pitts said, "it'll be quicker."

Sally and Lorne clung on to the frame of what turned out to be a four-seater beach buggy, and Pitts put his foot down. In his haste to get there, he almost tipped the vehicle over on its side as he rounded the corner too fast.

Sally swore under her breath. "We'd rather get there in one piece, Mr Pitts, if it's all the same to you."

"Sorry, it's always been a bit of a boy's toy for me. I forgot you ladies were on board with me."

Sally rolled her eyes, and she could tell Lorne was suppressing a snigger.

"Men," she mouthed.

The rest of the team, including Stuart and Jordan, were standing over Perry who was soaked from head to foot.

Sally pushed her way through. "We need blankets. Come on, guys, you know better than this. Don't just stand there, this man's life could be in danger."

"Someone has gone off to get them, boss," Jordan replied.

"Okay." Sally knelt beside Perry who had been placed in the recovery position. She watched his chest inflate and deflate rapidly. "At least he's alive. Where was he?" She glanced over her shoulder and saw a large cage on the dockside.

"He was in the cage; he'd been placed in the water. We found him unconscious," one of the younger officers said.

"At least he's alive. Although I think hypothermia has set in. The quicker we get those blankets..."

Another officer, carrying an armful of material, came hurtling around the corner of the nearby building towards them. "This is the best I could find." He threw the blankets on the ground beside Perry.

"They'll do. How far away is the ambulance, do we know?"

"I'll check, boss."

In the distance, a siren wailed.

"Don't bother, sounds like they're here. We don't want to delay them. Give the paramedics some room, move back." Sally shook out some of the blankets and covered Perry's body. He was out cold which was concerning, despite him breathing erratically.

The ambulance pulled up a few feet away, and the paramedics rushed towards them.

"Tell me what happened," the older one said.

"He was placed in a cage and submerged underwater."

"How long was he in the water?"

Sally waved her hand from side to side. "Hard to say, maybe fifteen to twenty minutes, but it might have been longer. We were tracing his movements on the cameras, but he went out of shot. He was being held captive by someone who kidnapped him. He was beaten up pretty badly before he was put in the car and brought to this location, if that helps."

"Great, yes, that's exactly what we need to know. Did he wake up at all? Spoken to anyone?"

"No, he's been unconscious all the time. His breathing, it's not the best, is it?"

The paramedic glanced up at her. "No. How long have the blankets been on him?"

"Seconds before you arrived."

"Thanks, right, you can leave us to it now, he's in safe hands."

Perry moaned and then gasped for breath.

"It's all right, mate. You're safe. We'll get you to hospital. Do you have any injuries?"

Perry's gaze flitted around the crowd and landed on Sally. "It was him. He did this. Have you caught him yet?"

"Not yet, Perry. Sorry this happened to you. Can you give us any information? Did he say why he abducted you?"

"Because he's a frigging moron. I can't believe he got away."

"He won't get far, I assure you."

"This is going to have to wait," the paramedic said. "We need to get this man to hospital. Rick, get the foil blanket, that'll get some heat into him quickly."

"Come on, let's give them room to work," Sally said. "I think we should continue the search of the area. He might still be here, watching what's going on. If you find anyone acting suspicious, hold on to him and give me a call right away."

The men split up and went off in different directions.

"Should we join the search?" Jordan asked.

"Yes, you do that. Lorne and I will head back to the car park, just in case he has the audacity to return to the car."

Pitts gave Sally and Lorne a lift back to the office. They remained inside, watching the car, but no one showed up.

"Come out, you bugger. I'm getting pissed off now."

"Keep calm," Lorne said. "If he's still around, he'll show himself soon enough. It'll be getting dark soon."

"Yep, that's what I'm worried about."

"Can I get you ladies a coffee while you wait?" Mr Pitts asked.

"That'd be great. White, one sugar for both, thank you."

He disappeared and returned with their drinks a few minutes later. "Here you go. I even found some Hobnobs in the cupboard. Help yourself."

"You're too kind. Have you run this company long?"

"I've worked on the docks most of my life, but only been in my position for the last couple of years."

"You must enjoy it, devoting all your life to your career."

"It has its good days and bad days, just like any other job, apparently." He leaned in close and lowered his voice. "It's a doddle most days, unlike your job, I should imagine."

"It has its moments." Something caught Sally's attention at the end of the car park. "Who is that?"

Lorne was out of the door before she could answer.

Sally slammed her mug down on the desk, spilling some of its contents. "Sorry, have to fly."

"Fingers crossed for you. Give him hell when you catch up with him."

Sally raised her thumb. She fished her mobile out of her pocket and rang Jordan. "We think we've spotted him. Get back to the car. Now."

She followed the route Lorne took, ducking down behind the cars immediately outside the office. They were within a few feet of the vehicle when Lorne broke cover.

"Christian Starr, stop right there."

Starr checked left and right and then bolted towards the main road. Lorne gave chase. Sally dropped back and jumped into the car instead. She rang Jordan again, apprised him of the situation.

"We're at the other end of the dock, boss. He'll be long gone by the time we get there."

Sally cursed. "Just do your best, Jordan."

She threw her mobile onto the passenger seat and drove to the exit. There was more traffic around, which she feared would probably go against them. Up ahead, she spotted Lorne darting between the cars. The man weaved between the passing cars, and still Lorne kept up the chase behind him.

"You go, girl. Nail the fucker."

The cars came to a standstill around her, and Sally watched on nervously as Lorne continued in her hunt for Christian. He ducked out of sight and popped up a couple of hundred yards ahead of Lorne. Sally could tell her partner was struggling to keep up the pace.

"Shit, I wish I could do something. Sod it, I can." She flung her car door open and ran towards them, aware that the other drivers would be cussing her for abandoning her car during rush hour on the busiest stretch of road for miles.

Lorne followed Christian over a nearby embankment. Sally seized the opportunity to get ahead of them, choosing to go around the slight incline instead, but she hadn't anticipated Christian changing tack. Suddenly, he was right in front of her, panic-stricken.

Sally held out her arms. "Let's be sensible about this, Christian, give yourself up."

"Why should I? What would be the point?"

Lorne leapt on his back, but he lashed out like a caged animal and upended her.

She landed with a thump and a groan. "Get him, Sal, don't let him get away."

"Catch me if you can," he teased.

And as Sally made her move, he darted to the side and took off in the other direction.

"Are you all right?"

"I'm fine. Be careful, Sal."

"Call the boys, tell them where we are. Get them to cut us off if they can," Sally shouted breathlessly.

She chased him up a narrow alley, praying that it wouldn't turn out to be a dead end, because she realised now, she was no match for him strength wise. However, she had speed on her side and felt relieved that she had chosen to wear a pair of flat shoes for work.

*Best idea you're going to have today, Sal, by the look of things.*

She came to a halt at the end of the alley. There were three obvious routes he could take. She slapped her hands against her thighs. "Damn you. Show me a sign, where are you?"

A scraping noise sounded to the right of her. She ran towards it and spotted Christian's leg disappearing over the top of the fence ahead of her. She knew, with her limited height, she would struggle to follow him, so Sally sprinted up the alley to the right which, at the end led to an open green area. With the light fading fast, she searched her surroundings, hoping to catch a glimpse, a movement that she could latch on to.

*Shit! Where are you?*

Frustration at an all-time high, Sally was on the verge of tears until something caught her attention to her left. She took a chance and ran in that direction. *It's him.* Luckily, he hadn't seen her. Had he presumed he'd given her the slip? She crouched behind a row of parked vehicles until she was around twenty feet away from him. As if sensing she was closing in on him, Christian peered over his shoulder and then bolted between the oncoming traffic.

Sally dashed after him, slapped the bonnet of a car travelling too fast and felt the wrath of the driver who blasted his horn and shouted a few choice expletives from his window. Sally gave him the finger by way of an apology but kept up her pace behind Christian until he slipped out of sight again.

She stopped and checked out the area once more. A few cars had come to a stop up ahead, and she wondered if he had something to do with the delay. Sally took a punt and bounded along the pavement towards the front of the queue, only to find a woman sitting on the edge of the road, her head in her hands, rocking back and forth. Two other women were comforting her.

Producing her warrant card, Sally asked, "Can I ask what happened?"

"That bastard… he took my car. Scared the shit out of me when he yanked my door open. He reached in, unhooked my seat belt, and then grabbed my arm. I tried to put up a fight, but he hit me in the face and then jumped into the driver's seat and sped off. The car is brand-new, to me anyway, it was a present from my boyfriend."

"I'm so sorry this has happened to you. Can you give me your registration number?"

The young woman chewed on her lip. "Shit, I don't know it. I haven't even filled it up with petrol yet, let alone anything else. How am I supposed to remember the reg?"

"Have you filled in the vehicle log and sent it back to DVLA?"

"Yes, the garage did that for me."

"Wait, which garage did he buy it from? And when?"

"Earlier today. Phil paid the garage owner in cash. It's the garage on Trident Street, not sure what it's called."

"Don't worry, I can sort that. Are you all right or do you need to go to hospital to get checked over?"

"No, I don't like to waste a doctor's time, they have enough on their plate. I'll be okay. I'll see if Phil will come and get me."

"Will he know the car details?"

She shrugged. "How do I know?"

"What's his number, and I'll give him a call?"

She searched around her and then thumped the side of her head. "I don't know, my phone was in my bag, and that's still in my car. Can't you do something?"

Sally smiled and stepped away to make a call. She rang the station, made the desk sergeant aware of the situation and requested a patrol car to attend. He told her that one would be with her within ten minutes.

Then Sally rang Lorne. "It's me. I lost him. I'm here near a park. He's hijacked someone's car. I'm going to need a lift."

"I can get Jordan to come and pick you up. What about the reg? Did you manage to get that? We can get things rolling on that front."

"No, and the woman who owns the car can't remember it."

"What the fuck?"

"In all fairness, her boyfriend only bought the car today."

"Ah, okay. We'll let her off in that case. What about the paperwork from the sale, or was it a private one?"

"Her boyfriend took care of it. The garage was on Trident Street. Odds are that they're closed now. So we're up shit creek."

"Leave it with me, I'll see what I can come up with. What's the woman's name and address?"

"Hang on." Sally wandered back to ask the young woman. "Can I have your name and address?"

"It's Gail Dodds. Three Montlake Road, King's Lynn."

Sally relayed the information to Lorne.

"I'll get back to you when I can."

"I've got a patrol car on the way to assist the woman. Ask Jordan to put his foot down, will you?"

"Impatient cow, he's on his way."

"Good. See you soon."

. . .

WITH THE OFFICERS now taking care of Miss Dodds, Sally and Jordan headed back to Sally's car. Angry drivers made their position clear as she climbed behind the wheel. She followed Jordan back to the dock area where Lorne and Stuart were going over the footage they had gone through earlier.

"That's an hour of my life I don't want to revisit anytime soon. Sorry for letting you down, guys. He's definitely got his wits about him."

"Sounds like he resorted to being a thug to get what he wants," Lorne said.

"Yep, the poor woman was really shaken up. Pissed off that her new car was stolen. Any news on the vehicle?"

"I managed to get the reg. Joanna is running it through the ANPR systems now. My take is that he'll dump it pretty soon and rob something else, just to keep ahead of us."

Sally tutted. "Yep, I thought the same. Anything here?"

"We're trying to find out who this other man is. Mr Pitts is going through the rotas to see who was in the area at the time. He shouldn't be long."

"That's great."

Mr Pitts entered the office waving a slip of paper in his hand. "I've managed to narrow it down to two men, and yes, I've checked and double-checked to ensure I have the right ones. Both men are off duty now, they finished about half an hour ago."

"That's great. We're going to need their home addresses, if you can oblige, Mr Pitts."

"Let me get that sorted for you now."

Sally held her fingers up. "We'll get both men interviewed while we're out here. After that, we'll make our way back to the station."

"One each?" Lorne asked.

"Makes sense. We'll cover the ground quicker."

Mr Pitts entered the room again and passed another sheet of paper to Sally.

"Jot this name and address down, Jordan," she said. "We'll take the other one."

THE TWO MEN lived a stone's throw from the dockyard, on the same road, in fact. Jordan and Stuart called at Mason Bronte's house while Sally and Lorne stopped off at Ed Durrant's.

He seemed surprised to see them standing on his doorstep. "The police, what do you want?" he asked after Sally had produced her warrant card.

"A word in private, if you don't mind."

"About what?"

"About the incident that happened down at the dock today. You were on duty down there, weren't you?"

"Yes, but I didn't see anything."

"Would it be all right if we came in and asked you a few questions?"

His eyes flickered shut, and he slammed the door back against the wall. "Do what you like. By the look of it, I don't have a frigging option, do I?"

Sally smiled. "Everyone has the option to do the right thing, Mr Durrant, or can I call you Ed?"

"Ed will do. Keep the noise down, the missus has just put the kids to bed."

*Shame you didn't consider the kids when you slammed the door against the wall.* "Is there somewhere else we can discuss this matter, rather than in the hallway?"

"Come through to the kitchen. The wife will be watching the soaps in the lounge. Maybe I should be grateful for you saving me that torture. I usually end up scrolling through my phone for a few hours."

He led them up the hallway to a room that was neat and homely. The sides were clear; someone in the home was houseproud, and she didn't think it would be him.

"Take a seat." He pulled out a pine chair, turned it around and straddled it.

Sally and Lorne sat in the couple of empty chairs opposite him. Lorne removed her notebook.

"Perhaps you can tell us what you witnessed today, down at the docks?" Sally asked, her tone light and enthusiastic, despite the late hour. It had been a very long day.

"I didn't see anything. Only you lot, milling around, or should that be hunting for someone?"

Sally wasn't in the mood for pussyfooting around so decided to go for the jugular. "Ah, now then, we have camera footage that proves the opposite is true. How well do you know Christian Starr?"

His gaze drifted towards the door and then back at Sally. "I don't."

"Come now. We have you on camera assisting him when he showed up at the docks with Perry Walters today, the man we rescued from a cage that had been placed in the water."

He shook his head over and over. "Not me. Are you sure about your facts?"

"Absolutely positive. If you'd rather take this down the station, the choice is yours."

"No, I can't leave here, not tonight. My wife is ill."

Sally frowned and tilted her head. "Oh, what's wrong with her? Funny, you never mentioned that before."

"She's got a stinking cold and is the world's worst when she's ill. She's in the lounge now, tucked up in the duvet, watching the soaps. I just left that part out when I told you she was watching TV before."

"Ah, DS Warner, would you mind checking to see if Mrs

Durrant is all right or if she needs anything to make her more comfortable?"

Lorne pushed back her chair and stood. "I'll be right back."

"No. Jesus, all right, all right, I'll tell you what I know. If you promise to keep Trisha out of it."

"Trisha? Is that your wife?"

"Yes. She'd be mortified to learn that I had anything to do with what happened today."

"And what did happen, Ed?"

Lorne flipped open her notebook and started scribbling.

"I got conned, that's what."

"Conned, how?"

"I received a call from Christian, asking if I could help him get out of a 'fix' he was in. I said I'd do my best. He shouted and told me if I didn't help him, he'd come round here and tell my wife…"

"Tell your wife about what?"

"That I owe him a lot of money."

"A lot?"

"Twenty grand. It was an old gambling debt that Christian helped me pay off a couple of years ago, before he disappeared."

"Are you telling me that you've been complicit in his deception?"

"Deception, if that's what you want to call it. Like I said, he had a metaphoric knife held to my throat. I've been living on eggshells for years, waiting for him to get in touch and demand his money back. That call came the other day. Well, not for the money, but he told me he needed a favour. When I asked what type of favour, he said he wanted to teach someone a lesson and needed me to assist him to pull his plan together down at the dockyard. I swear I tried to get out of it, but he has this hold over me. I can't afford to pay him back the funds, so he said he was willing to write off half the debt if I helped him out. What would you do in my shoes?"

Sally shrugged. "The right thing, call the police and make them aware of the situation. There are ways around every problem, especially if a person's life is at stake."

He ran a hand through his hair and then around his face. "I didn't know what he was going to do. I wouldn't have allowed the man to have stayed in there for long, I promise."

"Is that right? And what would you have done, eventually?"

"Given an anonymous tip-off to the police."

"And you expect us to believe you?"

"It's the truth. I've never hurt anyone in my life before. If, as you say you have, seen the footage, you'll see me reluctantly helping him."

Sally nodded. "Yes, we noted there was a degree of hesitancy on your part. Why didn't you stick to your values and walk away?"

"Bloody hell, are you not listening? He threatened my damn family. You find me a man who wouldn't comply when he has that over his head."

Sally waved her hand from side to side. "Depends if Christian has always come across as a dangerous man to you or not. Has he?"

"No, never, but there was something sinister lingering in his eyes. He's a changed man. He's not the man I went to college with, that's how long I've known him. When you see something like that you begin to question what that person is capable of. You'd have to, right?"

"I suppose. So, you say you've been in touch with him since he disappeared. Where has he been?"

"Around."

Sally shook her head. "You're going to need to do better than that. Around where?"

"Not far from his home. He has always kept an eye on Zara and his daughter."

"What? Why? Why let them believe that something bad had happened to him?"

"Ask him, not me. I've never been able to get an answer out of him."

"Have you seen the news this week? The appeal I've personally put out for him to come forward?"

His brow wrinkled into a deep frown. "No, I never really watch the news. The missus is the one with her finger on the remote control every night."

Sally rolled her eyes. "Do you know who the man was whose life you helped put in danger today?"

"No, he never said, but I thought I recognised him. We didn't have time to hang around and have a conversation, he wanted to get down to business there and then. Who was he?"

"His brother-in-law, Zara's brother."

"Shit. Yes, that's right. I met him on their wedding day. He had more hair back then, I should have realised. He was pleading with me to help him as if he knew me. Maybe he recognised me. Hell, what was Christian thinking?"

"That's what we'd like to know."

"If he's prepared to do that kind of shit to a member of his family…" He paused and shook his head. "See, I told you, there was a look in his eye that unsettled me. He forced me into helping him, you have to believe me. As much as I love him, he's unhinged."

"And yet you thought it was all right for him to walk away from his family and start afresh?"

"Well, if you put it like that, yeah, I suppose that was a crap thing to do."

"Why didn't you challenge him about it? Try to get the

truth out of him over the past few years? Persuade him to return home even?"

His chin dipped to his chest, and he swallowed. "I couldn't bring myself to do it."

"Why?" Sally observed him closely and suspected he was withholding something important.

"I just couldn't. He was—sorry, is—my mate. True friends support their mates, not spend all their time urging them to do the right thing. He had his reasons for doing what he did. Maybe we should all learn to respect his wishes and get on with life."

"You think? Maybe your conscience will allow you to do that, but mine definitely won't. If you didn't see my appeal go out, let me inform you what it was about. His daughter, Mila, is very sick in hospital at present."

"Shit! I didn't know, he never said anything to me. What's wrong with her?"

"She's in desperate need of a kidney transplant before it's too late."

"You mean she's going to die if she doesn't get one?"

"Correct. Now do you understand why we urgently need to find him?"

"I can. Fuck, if he knew she was ill then why would he go after his brother-in-law like that? How's that going to help Mila?"

"You took the words out of my mouth. More to the point, he doesn't seem to be in any hurry to help his daughter either."

"Do you think he saw the appeal when it went out?"

"Don't you? Why else would he go after Perry after all this time?"

"Shit! What the fuck is he up to? He loves his daughter more than anyone else in this world. I know if it was down to him that he'd be there in a heartbeat to help her."

"If it were down to him? What are you saying?"

He gulped and closed his eyes, mumbled an expletive and shook his head. "Oh no, did I say that? Poor choice of words on my part, sorry."

Sally stared at him, long and hard, but he purposely avoided looking at her. "Why do I get the feeling that you're still holding something back from us?"

"I'm not, I promise. I've told you everything I know and more, you have to believe me, it's the truth."

"Does Trisha know Christian?"

"No, not really. She's heard me talking about him, but we've not been together that long."

"How old are your kids?"

"Five and seven. They're hers, from a previous relationship."

"Ah, okay. Going back to Christian, do you know where he lives?"

He shuffled in his seat and remained silent.

"I've had enough of this. Either you speak openly with us, or we take you in for questioning and possibly charge you with attempted murder."

"What the fuck? You can't do that. I haven't done anything wrong."

"Then start bloody talking."

"I can tell you roughly where he lives. I can't remember the actual house number."

"Go on. Wait, would you be able to take us to the door?"

"I don't think so. It's towards the bottom end of Chapel Street in Dereham."

Sally and Lorne shared a knowing glance. If memory served her right, it was in the vicinity of the shop where the witness had stated seeing him and very close to where Zara and Mila lived.

"Sounds plausible. What else can you tell us about him? Does he work?"

"He flits between jobs, can't seem to hold anything down lately. I suppose it's tough getting back into the market once you've run your own business. He came looking for a job around the docks, but there was nothing going at my firm at the time. The boss took his name down and promised to get back to him if anything came up."

"Right, is he with someone else?"

He shrugged and avoided eye contact again.

"Do you have a phone number for him? Does he drive a car?"

"I have a mobile for him. Yes, I can give you that, but I wouldn't ring it, not unless you want him to go on the run again."

Sally grinned. "Grant me with more sense than that." She knew that they would be able to trace his whereabouts on the phone, if it was turned on. "What about a car?"

"No, I think he had an old one, but it broke down a few months back and he hasn't got around to getting a new one."

"He's been stealing cars, hasn't he?"

"He might have been, who knows?"

Ed left the table and walked over to the worktop where his mobile was lying, close to the kettle. He read the number out, and Lorne jotted it down, then he returned to his seat, choosing to sit on the chair correctly this time.

"Is that it?" he asked.

"Yes, for now. We'll still need you to visit the station to give us a statement, the sooner the better."

"Am I in trouble?"

"It depends."

"On what?"

"On whether the information you've given us this evening turns out to be true or not."

"It's the truth. I swear it is."

"It better be, otherwise we'll have no other option than to fling the book at you."

"But I didn't do anything wrong, not really."

"You were an accomplice to a very serious crime."

"Shit! Why did he have to involve me in this? I've never done anything against the law before. I could do without this shit, especially with Trisha ill in there."

"We'll take into consideration the information you've divulged this evening, don't worry. I'm fair when people show willing to do the right thing."

His eyes widened, and he shuffled forward like an eager puppy. "Thank you, honestly, I've tried my very best to tell you everything tonight."

"Which we appreciate. We'll leave you to enjoy the rest of your evening now. I'll give you one of my cards. Call me if anything else should come to mind."

"I will. I promise." He showed them to the front door.

"A word of caution, Ed, don't be tempted to warn him that we're on his tail, it'll only go against you."

"I won't. What he did today was wrong. If I had any balls, I would have prevented that guy going into the water. I feel ashamed I let it happen, believe me."

"Fortunately, Perry survived the incident. This would be a different visit entirely if he hadn't."

"Good luck. Be gentle with Christian, I think he's pretty mixed up about life in general at the moment."

"I'm sorry, but our sympathy has to remain with his daughter. Any man worth his weight should be stepping up to save her."

He nodded. "I agree. If he calls me, I'll make out I saw the appeal and urge him to come forward, if that will help?"

"It will, massively. Thanks."

They walked back to the car.

"Where to now?" Lorne asked.

"I'm done in. I've toyed with the idea of going round there to see if we can locate his house, but if he clocks us, I think that might make him go on the run again. Therefore, I think it's best if we leave it until the morning. We'll trace his phone, see what comes from that, and then make our move. We'll take Stuart and Jordan with us as backup."

Lorne tutted. "I know what you're saying makes a lot of sense, but there's a part of me that wants to go round there and haul his arse into a cell overnight."

Sally smiled. "Patience, partner. Our chance will come. You never know, he might be sitting in the reception area at the station in the morning, waiting for us, willing to do the right thing by his family."

Lorne pointed at the cloudy sky. "And there goes another one of those pink creatures with trotters and a squished snout."

"Get in. Let's get home. While I sign the Taser back in, can you ring ahead, let the boys know we're on our way? With any luck, Tony might have cleaned the kennels for you."

Lorne snorted. "I won't be holding my breath on that one. Want me to check the hospital as well? See if Perry is okay?"

"That'd be great, save me a job later."

Sally considered the conversation they'd had with Ed Durrant while Lorne made the calls, wondering if she had missed something obvious.

"Did you hear me?" Lorne jabbed her in the ribs.

"What? Sorry, no. Say again?"

"Simon is asking if you fancy an Indian or Chinese tonight? He doesn't feel like cooking and is willing to pop out for one."

"Indian would be preferable. Yes, that's got the saliva wreaking havoc."

"Eew… did you hear that, Simon? You've got her salivating already... I'll tell her you said that." Lorne laughed and ended the call.

"Go on, spill. What did the comic genius have to say in response?"

Lorne remained tight-lipped and shook her head. "Not going there. You can get it out of him when you apply your cuffs to the headboard later."

Sally laughed and tutted. "Behave yourself, we're not teenagers in the first throes of lust."

"You mean it's not normal for couples to tie each other up? Oops..."

"As if you and Tony get up to that kind of crap."

"My lips are sealed. What goes on in the bedroom at our house stays in the bedroom."

"Bloody hell, that's shocked me."

Lorne sniggered. "It was meant to, numpty. I'm just messing with you."

"You know what they say, many a true word spoken in jest."

## CHAPTER 9

The team all showed up for work the next day eager to get on with things. In fact, Sally had to rein them in before their morning meeting.

"I'm keen to do this by the book, guys. I sense we're going to get one shot at it. We all know what a great escape artist he is. Let's tamper down our enthusiasm and make him pay, in the right way."

The team all agreed, and they spent the next fifteen minutes going over things that might stand in their way and how they could overcome them.

"Would it be better to set up surveillance, in his road at least?" Jordan asked.

"We need to see what his phone brings up, trace the number to give us a location. My guess is that he will either be at the house or close by. He doesn't appear to wander far from familiar settings. Joanna's already made a start on that. Any news on the car stolen last night?"

Stuart picked up the phone. "I'll ring the garage now."

"Good. It might be a case of too little too late, but if he's still got hold of the car, tracing it through the cameras could be our key to finding him, if he's using another hideout."

"I'm going to check the electoral roll, see if his name or something similar crops up on that," Lorne said.

"We might as well cover all the bases. Let me know how you get on as soon as anything comes your way, folks. I'll be in my office, going through the usual crap."

Sally took a coffee with her to tackle her daily mind-numbing chore and paused at the window to admire the view that was far-reaching in the morning sun.

THIRTY MINUTES LATER, with the chores out of the way, she rejoined her team. "Any news?"

"The car was found dumped. When I checked the area, it turned out to be close to Chapel Street."

Sally rubbed her hands. "I do love it when a plan comes together. What about the electoral roll, Lorne, anything there?"

"Nothing as yet, no."

"One more brief point of note," Jordan began.

Sally nodded, encouraging him to reveal all.

"The shop where the witness thought she'd seen him is at the top end of Chapel Street."

"Winner, winner, chicken dinner. Okay, I've heard enough, let's get this party started. Joanna, if you find out anything else, give me a call. Come on, guys, let's go and bag ourselves a missing person-cum-attempted murderer. Talking of which, Lorne, can you check in with the hospital en route, see how the three patients are all doing?"

"Sure thing."

Sally led the way down the concrete stairs, Lorne, Stuart and Jordan close behind her. "You carry on, I'm going to sign out a Taser, just in case."

Once she was armed, she continued out to the car. She motioned for Jordan that she would take the lead. "How are the patients getting on?"

"Mila had a rough night, wanted to be with her mum, but they managed to sedate her. Perry is due to be discharged this morning, and Zara had an okay night but continues to be concerned about her daughter, for obvious reasons."

"Yeah, I think that would be me, too. Hopefully, by the end of the day we'll have some good news for them that could turn all their lives around."

"I hope that's not a case of wishful thinking on your part."

"There's only one way to find out." Sally started the engine and eased out of the car park. The traffic was moving steadily, and within thirty minutes the small convoy had arrived in Chapel Street. Sally drew up outside the shop and hopped out. "I won't be a sec."

She entered the grocer's and walked up to the young Chinese girl behind the counter. "Hi, I wonder if you can help me."

"Of course, what you need?" The woman thankfully spoke good English.

Sally withdrew her warrant card and her mobile. She scrolled through to the picture she had of Christian. "Do you know this man?"

The shop assistant nodded and smiled eagerly. "Ah, yes, ah, yes, that's Mr Henson. He nice man. Always pleasant, I never have no trouble from him."

Sally smiled. "Do you happen to know where he lives?"

"Yes, yes. He lives in last house, at the bottom of the road." She frowned as she thought. "The one on the right."

"Do you know if he's lived there long?"

"Maybe eighteen months to two years. With his wife and daughter."

At first Sally thought the shop assistant must have been

mistaken, but the more she thought about it, the more things began to add up.

*The bastard has been leading a double life. Changed his name in the process as well. What the fuck? Well, I'm afraid your lies have caught up with you, Christian, it's called the nature of the beast.*

Not that she'd come across many like this in the past. "I appreciate your help, thanks very much."

"No problem, always pleasure to help the police. We good people."

"You have a very nice business here, take care."

She marched past her own car to relay the information to Jordan and Stuart. "We'll approach the house cautiously. The last thing we want to do is scare the shithead into going on the run again. We'll take the front, you two keep an eye on the back." She returned to her car and smiled at Lorne. "We've got him, he's living under a new name which is probably why he didn't show up on the roll. He's also married and has a daughter."

"Fucking tosser. Yet another life he's messed up in the process."

Sally laughed. "Don't hold back, partner."

"Sorry, but what gives him, or anyone else for that matter, the right to ditch one family when the going gets tough, just to start on another one?"

"I can't answer that. Hopefully we'll get to the bottom of it when we catch up with him, which could be imminently. Are you ready for this?"

Lorne ground her fist into the palm of her other hand. "Let me at him."

"Easy tiger."

Sally drove to the bottom of the road and parked in a space close to the house. Jordan slotted in behind her, and their two colleagues jumped in the back of Sally's car.

"We'll sit here and observe for a few minutes then split up," Sally said. "Can anyone see any movement?"

"Nothing so far," Lorne confirmed. "Wait, there, at the upstairs window."

A woman holding a baby pulled back the curtains to the smaller of the two windows, overlooking the street.

Sally nodded. "At least we know someone is at home. Let's make our move."

Jordan and Stuart got out of the vehicle and casually walked past the house, deep in conversation as a ruse, and snuck down the alley at the side.

Sally checked her Taser, and once she was out of the car, tucked it into her belt at the back of her trousers. "A tad uncomfortable. Remind me not to sit down if we're offered a seat."

Lorne grinned. "Rather you than me." She rapped on the door after having no success with the doorbell.

The woman, still holding the baby, answered the door and jiggled the child on her hip. "Hello, can I help?"

Sally flashed her warrant card along with a cheesy smile. "Mrs Henson?"

The woman's gaze flitted between them. "Yes. Why would the police come calling at my door? Have I done something wrong?"

"Not in the slightest. Is your husband home?"

"No, he's gone out. He's on duty this afternoon, so he's nipped to the supermarket for me to get a few essentials that I need for the baby. Why? What's he done wrong?"

"Oh, nothing. We just wanted to have a brief chat with him about a case we're investigating. Would it be all right if we come in and wait for him?"

"I don't see why not, I've got nothing to hide."

Sally smiled, and the woman walked backwards into the hallway, where she paused at the bottom of the stairs.

"I've only just got the little one up, so my day hasn't really started yet, and you'll have to forgive me if the house is a mess. Always difficult keeping on top of things with a one-year-old glued to you most of the day."

"I can imagine. What's she called?"

"Fiona. Little Fi, we call her. She's adorable ninety percent of the time. The other ten percent it's like living with Jekyll and Hyde, you don't know what you're going to get from one day to the next."

"That's what makes it fun, isn't it? A little one keeping you on your toes."

"Debatable at best. Depends if you're on the receiving end of one of her tantrums or not."

"Does hubby help out? Or is he a 'hands off' kind of father?"

"He does what he can. His shifts can be a bit up and down and all over the place. I think he'd willingly help out more if he could."

"What does he do for a living?"

"Whatever he can lay his hands on at the moment. He's had a few jobs over the last couple of years, but none of them have suited him. And yes, we've had the conversation about settling down with regular hours now Fiona is with us, but it's such a struggle these days to find a good job. I would suggest that I went back to work at the salon, if I knew he was up to the task and she'd be in safe hands. Ouch, that sounded bad the way it came out. I'm not saying that he would ever hurt the baby, far from it. What I was trying to put across is that a mother's instinct about her child is hard to ignore and something that is difficult to explain to a partner."

Sally nodded. "I understand that completely. Do you know when your husband is likely to be back?"

"Within the next ten to fifteen minutes. You've got me

intrigued. Why do you want to see him? Come through to the kitchen, I'll make you a drink after I've prepared Fiona's porridge for her. She rejected it earlier, she only really eats when she's hungry, which isn't a bad thing, I suppose. Although it frustrates the hell out of me most of the time."

"Babies can be a law unto themselves at that age," Lorne chipped in.

"Tell me it gets better as they get older."

Lorne groaned. "I'd be lying if I said it did. It tends to get harder, I'm afraid."

"Oh crap. Now you're going to tell me it's worth all the angst, aren't you?"

Lorne grinned. "Sometimes. No, I'm joking, the love between a parent and a child is very special. Enjoy every minute of it."

"Oh, I intend to. That's why I'm reluctant to swap roles with Adam."

"Sorry, I didn't catch your name," Sally said.

"It's Laila."

"Have you been married long?"

"Two years now, although we've been together four years."

"Is this a picture of him?" Sally walked towards the far wall to get a closer look at the family photo. Christian had changed his appearance slightly. His hair was shorter and seemed to be lighter.

"Yes, it was taken not long after I had Fiona, hence me still looking nine months pregnant."

"You appear to be content and extremely happy," Sally said.

"I was, I mean I am. Oops, major slip of the tongue there."

"Was it? Is everything all right between you and your husband?"

Laila frowned and placed Fiona in her highchair at the table. "Why do you ask?"

"A simple question. I know what a strain a new baby can put on a relationship."

"No strain. He's here when I need him. Better than most men, isn't it? Some of my friends' partners buggered off and left them as soon as the baby came along."

"Sorry to hear that. It can be a nightmare bringing up a baby on your own."

"I hope I never get to find out. Tea or coffee?"

"Coffee for both of us, milk and one sugar, thank you," Sally replied. "What about your family, do you get much support from them?"

"My family are all down south. Sadly, Adam's parents are no longer with us, they both died of cancer a few years ago."

"Sorry to hear that. It's always good to have a family to support you when you've recently had a child."

"My friends have rallied around when we needed them." Laila prepared their drinks. "Take a seat. Can I tempt you with a shortbread biscuit? I made them myself yesterday. They come with a warning attached, they're super moreish."

"Why not? Sod the waistline," Sally said. She was warming to this woman and knew that the news about her husband, when it finally came out, would devastate her, especially being a newish mother.

Drinks made and with some star-shaped shortbreads lying on a plate in the middle of the table, Sally discreetly removed her Taser and placed it on the chair behind her and covered it with her jacket. She tucked into a biscuit and moaned with pleasure. "You weren't wrong, these are lovely. Can you tell us where Adam is from?"

"The London area, not sure which part. I recall him telling me that he used to walk along the embankment every day on his way into work."

"What job did he have down there?" Sally knew it was all a lie, but she was intrigued to know what tale he'd spun Laila and how deep his lies had gone.

"Something in the city. I think he was a trader. Moved up here to get away from all the hustle and bustle of the city."

"How did you meet?"

"At a pub one night. He was out with some friends on a boys' night out and he zeroed in on me. He told me I had a smile that lit up the room. I thought it was codswallop and corny at the time, but the more I went out with him, the more I realised what a genuine man he was."

Sally gulped and stared at the photo once more. "He seems a really nice man."

"He is. I was existing until he swept into my life and captured my heart."

"A romantic, is he?"

Laila smiled, and her cheeks coloured up. "He can be. He took me to Paris as a surprise, and that's where he proposed."

"How wonderful." Sally's gaze dropped to the large solitaire sitting prominently on Laila's left hand. Time was running out, if, as Laila had assumed, Adam would be back soon. Sally needed to broach the subject of him leading a double life. She took a sip from her coffee and nibbled at her biscuit, then pushed it away as it lodged in her throat. "Laila, there's something we need to tell you before Adam returns."

Laila paused feeding Fiona and stared at her. "What's that? Has he done something bad?"

Sally shrugged. "It depends on your definition of bad."

"Now you're worrying me. Please, don't keep me in suspense. If you have something to say, just spit it out, preferably before he gets home."

"Have you seen the news this week?"

"No, I think I've been too busy with Fiona to sit and

watch any TV over the past couple of days. Why? What have I missed?"

Sally removed her mobile from her pocket and angled the photo of Christian towards Laila. "Do you recognise him?"

Little Fiona started coughing, and Laila's attention was drawn back to her daughter. "There, there, Mummy's here, sweetie. All better now. Take a sip of your drink."

"Did you get a close look at him?" Sally asked.

"Why don't I take over feeding the baby?" Lorne suggested.

"No, she doesn't like strangers feeding her. And no, I didn't get a long enough look at the photo. Show it to me again."

Sally offered Laila her phone to take. Laila frowned and glanced up at Sally.

"Who is this? I mean, it looks like my husband, but I don't think it's him. Who is it?"

"His name is Christian Starr."

"Right, and who is he? And what does he have to do with me and my family?" Panic rose in her tone.

"We believe Christian and Adam are the same person. Admittedly, Adam's hair is lighter; do you know if he uses a tint on it?"

"I think so. But... who? Why? I'm confused. Who is this Christian? Should I even be asking that? Do I want to know? I don't understand, how can he be two people at the same time?"

"That's what we're interested to know. Christian Starr went missing two years ago. He has a wife and a teenage daughter."

"What? Are you crazy? Shit! There must be some mistake. There has to be. We'll have this sorted when Adam gets home. I should ring him."

"No, please, don't do that. We nearly caught up with your husband yesterday, but he escaped us."

"Escaped you? Sorry for repeating what you're saying all the time, but I'm having difficulty comprehending what the heck is going on here. What's your visit really about?"

"We need to question your husband, Adam, otherwise known as Christian, about several incidents that have come to our attention lately."

Laila's gaze shifted between Lorne, who was trying to coax Fiona to eat her porridge, and Sally. "I'm at a loss here. Please, you're not making any sense. What has Adam done?" Tears surfaced, and a stray one dripped onto her cheek.

"Yesterday, he attempted to kill his brother-in-law."

"No way! That's a lie. This is a nightmare, you must have it wrong."

"I'm sorry if this has come as a shock to you, but we believe Adam turned his back on his other family probably with the intention of setting up home with you."

"Why? I need to have this out with him. I need to call him, now."

"No, please don't. Wait for him to come home and face the truth. You need to hear it from his lips. There's more."

"Shit! I don't want to hear it." Laila slapped her hands over her ears.

Sally reached over and pulled her hands away. "Please, it's important that you hear all the facts before he gets home."

Sobbing, Laila said, "You're breaking my heart with these lies. Please, stop it."

"You have to believe me, they're not lies. It's the truth as we know it and has been corroborated by several people."

"You might as well tell me everything, but I bet he disputes it when he gets back."

"Maybe. A friend of mine asked me to look into a cold case as I head up a specific team. A mutual friend, called Zara

Starr, told me her husband, Christian, went missing two years ago. There was no rhyme or reason for him taking off. Anyway, earlier this week, I put out a plea for Christian to come forward for the sake of his daughter. Since then, he's been cropping up here and there."

Laila raised a hand to stop Sally saying anything else. "Back up. Why for the sake of his daughter?"

"Mila is sixteen now and is seriously ill in hospital."

"Oh heck. Can you tell me what's wrong with her?"

"Her kidneys are failing, and she's in desperate need of an organ donation. Her mother is too poorly to offer her one of hers, and the rest of the family have been tested, but none of them are a good match."

"And that leaves the father… this Christian, or Adam as I know him?" Laila shook her head over and over. "This is like something out of a cheap B-movie. Jesus, you then went on to say he keeps cropping up. Can you explain what that means?"

"He appeared in Zara's hospital room a few days ago, and yesterday he attempted to kill her brother."

"Zara, that's the mother, right?" Laila asked.

"Yes."

"I don't understand, why is she in hospital?"

"Because when we paid her a visit the other day, she was skin and bone and in dire straits. My partner and I took her to A and E. She was admitted straight away and has been there ever since."

"Good grief. Why did she allow herself to get into such a state in the first place?"

"The pressure of dealing with her husband's disappearance. They used to run a business together. He left her with huge debts, took out loans in her name and, it would seem, all the while he was leading a double life with you, behind her back."

"No, no. We can't be talking about the same man, not my Adam."

"It's the truth."

"What do you want from me? I had nothing to do with any of this. You're not going to arrest me, are you?"

"No, we can tell you're an innocent party..." Sally paused to glance at her mobile which was ringing for the second time. "to your husband's shambolic behaviour. Sorry, I need to get this." She unlocked the back door and stepped outside, closing it behind her. "Jordan, what's up?"

"We spotted him the same time as he saw us. He took off and is on the run again."

"Shit! Have you got him in your sights?"

"We lost him. Sorry, boss. We're trawling the nearby streets, trying to locate him."

"Have you called for backup?"

"Yes, they're on their way, but we both know how proficient he is at evading capture."

"I know, do your best. Keep me informed." Sally kicked out at the brick wall in front of her, instantly regretting her decision when she managed to stub her little toe.

She pushed open the back door. Laila and Lorne both turned her way.

"It wasn't good news. Adam showed up and saw our colleagues outside."

"Have they arrested him?" Laila asked.

"No. He ran off... again."

"Bugger," Lorne cursed.

"Backup is on the way."

Laila failed to hold back the tears, and her head collapsed onto her arms spread out on the table in front of her. This had a devastating effect on Fiona who saw her mother in a desperate state. Lorne shrugged, obviously out of her comfort zone.

Sally tried to soothe Laila with calming words, but the woman's emotions tipped over the edge.

"I can't... I don't know what I've done to deserve this. I've always been a decent person, never wronged anyone, not as far as I can remember, only to be conned, to be cheated by someone I thought I could trust. I don't think I'll ever get past this."

Sally felt numb, unsure what to suggest to make the woman feel better, until a lightbulb went off in her mind. "Are you willing to help us?"

Laila sat up and wiped away her tears with the sleeve of her jumper. "Yes, I'll do anything you want. I need to put things right, I'm that sort of person."

"Okay, will you come back to the station with us? And if I can organise a press conference, will you make a plea for him to come forward?"

"That's a brilliant idea," Lorne said enthusiastically.

"Yes, yes, I'll do it. I'm going to be scared shitless, being in front of the camera, but I'll do it, if only to try and put things right. What is he thinking? Running off when his family, his *other family*, need him? I need him. I need to know if this is all true. Why he's deceived me all these years. I thought he loved me. Clearly, I was wrong."

"I can't answer that. If he's never knowingly treated you badly, maybe he does love you. We won't know what's going on in that head of his until we find him."

"I have so many questions I want to ask him. I just don't know how I feel about him any longer. How can I love him after what he's done to me?"

Sally rubbed her arm. "None of this is your fault. It's not like you knew he was married and you were carrying on behind the other woman's back."

"No, because I would never do that, ever. I've always

thought of mistresses, women who set their sights on men who were already married, as being the lowest of the low."

"You mustn't think that way. Adam's deception is his downfall, this is no reflection on you. Can we set off soon? I realise you'll have to pack a bag for Fiona et cetera."

"That won't take long, I have one permanently packed for when we nip out anyway. Give me two minutes to put something decent on." She glanced down at the ripped jeans and T-shirt she was wearing.

"You sort yourself out and, between us, we'll try to feed Fiona."

"You're going to need all the luck in the world." Laila smiled and ran out of the room.

"I can handle the baby, if you want to get in touch with Georgia about the conference," Lorne suggested.

"You're a star." Sally rang the station and was put through to the press officer who was only too happy to help out.

"How long will you be?"

"I should imagine max thirty minutes," Sally responded.

"Great, I'll see if I can get one organised within the hour, it's been done before."

"That would be amazing. See you soon. Ring me when you can."

"Leave it with me. I hope it helps bring him in, Sally."

"You and me both."

## CHAPTER 10

Laila was a real trooper the whole time she was at the station. She never wavered throughout her appeal, speaking from the heart that her husband had ripped to shreds. Her final plea silenced the room of hard-nosed journalists and brought a tear to most of their eyes.

"Please, Adam, do the right thing. We forgive you, Fiona and I. You'll always be the person I fell in love with, no matter what's gone on already. Do it for us, but more importantly, do it for Mila, she needs you. Without you coming forward, she'll die. Could you live with yourself, knowing that you let her die unnecessarily? Darling, Adam, come in from the cold. Give yourself up. You're not a selfish person, you never have been. Please, I'm trusting you to do what's right, for us, for all your family."

Sally cleared the massive lump from her throat with a subtle cough and thanked the journalists for attending at such short notice. Then she and Georgia led Laila back into the anteroom where Little Fi was waiting for her with Lorne.

Laila picked up her daughter and snuggled into the soft,

warm folds of her chubby little neck. "Let's hope Daddy comes back to us soon, sweetheart. We miss him so much, don't we?"

"If your heartfelt plea doesn't hit the mark, Laila, then nothing will. You were amazing up there. A natural before the camera," Sally commended her.

"I spoke from the heart, just like any other woman would have done in my situation. I could do with a coffee as a reward after my exertions. What happens now?"

"I wouldn't normally allow it and I might need to run it past my senior officer, but I think you and Fiona should stay with us, for now at least, until I can arrange a safe house for you."

She gasped. "What? Do you think he'll harm us?"

Sally sighed and shrugged. "Let's put it this way, everything he's done so far has blindsided us. Who knows what the hell is going through that head of his? Humour me, please?"

Fresh tears emerged and dribbled on to Laila's ruddy cheeks. "When I woke up this morning, beside my loving husband, I hasten to add, I never dreamed this would be how my day would turn out."

"I know. I'm so sorry. Maybe the day will have a perfect ending, for everyone concerned."

"I hope so, for all our sakes. Have you heard how Mila is?"

"Not recently. I can make the call to the hospital once we're upstairs. Let me get in touch with my DCI, get the all-clear from him, and then I'll gladly sort you out with the coffee you're in dire need of." Sally left the room and rang her boss.

DCI Green listened attentively as Sally movingly put her point across as to why Laila should remain within close proximity of the team, before he asked, "And at the end of your shift? What then, Inspector? Will you make sure the woman and her child are safe by allowing them to stay at your house for the night, too?"

"Yes. If I have to, sir. She deserves to be treated well, they both do."

"Hmm... very well. It's clear to me that you've made your mind up about this one whether I give the go-ahead or not, am I correct?"

"Me, go against your wishes or a direct order, sir? Never, that's unthinkable. I think you must have me mixed up with another inspector at the station."

"And sarcasm is only going to make matters worse. Do what you have to do to keep them safe, but more importantly, I need you to get uniform involved, ensure this man is arrested ASAP."

"That's my intention, sir. I appreciate you giving me the authority to do that."

He grunted and hung up, probably sensing that she had hoodwinked him, yet again.

She punched the air and returned to the room to share the news. "When will the first airing be, Georgia, do you know?"

"The local radio stations told me their plan is to get something on air within the next hour. I'll make sure I have the radio on to check."

"Thanks for all your help in pulling this together so quickly. You've definitely gone above and beyond on this one."

"My pleasure." Georgia faced Laila and smiled. "And all you have to do is sit in a warm police station and take care of this little one. I'm jesting, of course. I know how difficult this situation must be for you, but I want to assure you, you've got the right team by your side. Sally and Lorne are seasoned pros who always put the people willing to assist them, first."

"Thank you," Laila said and hugged Fiona tighter.

"You say the nicest things," Sally said, feeling emotional. "Right, we'd better get you upstairs and settled, Laila. Can you do the honours, Lorne? I want to stop off at reception, ask Pat if he'll assign more patrols to the search."

"Consider it done. Come on, Laila, I'll grab your bag."

TEN MINUTES LATER AND, with the extra patrols organised with Pat, Sally climbed the stairs to the office. Lorne had settled Laila and Fiona in an area near the drinks station. They both appeared to be happy to be there. Sally couldn't help wondering how long that would last. She had a brief chat with every member of the team about their need for discretion and to hold their tongue if any news came their way until they relocated to Sally's office to share the information.

"Everything all right, Laila?"

"Thank you, Inspector. One thing, if I may be so bold?"

"Name it."

"Is it possible for us to listen to the appeal being aired on the radio? I'd like to hear if they edited it much before putting it out there."

"I can arrange it. In all honesty, I feel sure they wouldn't have either the time or the inclination to alter anything, and why would they? It was perfect the way it was. Believe me, if you can affect a roomful of journalists like that, I'm sure Adam will make the right call and come forward."

"I hope so. I've always considered him to be an honourable man."

"Good. Let's hope you're right. Please, shout if you need anything. Help yourself to drinks as and when you want one. Despite the impression you probably get from the TV about the police, we don't tend to sit around all day, drinking endless cups of coffee, but it is always on hand."

"I can't thank you enough, honestly."

"I'll get one of the lads to nip out for sandwiches a bit later on, time permitting."

Laila nodded and picked up one of Fiona's soft, squidgy teddy bears that she had brought with her. "This will keep her amused for hours."

Sally moved around the room to Lorne's desk. "Can you get the news on the radio for me? Laila wants to hear the appeal go out, for herself."

"I'll do that. What do you think our chances are for the rest of the day?"

"Slim to narrow, you?"

"About the same. Let's hope hearing Laila's voice either on the radio or on the TV will have the desired effect on him and forces him to do the right thing for his family."

"We can but hope. I'll be in my office. I want to ring the hospital, check everything is still okay there. Will you keep on top of things out here? Organise lunch for everyone. I'll get Laila's and Fiona's out of petty cash."

"That's the least of our worries, leave it with me."

Sally wandered into her office and closed the door behind her. She leaned her head against it and breathed out the largest of sighs. "Come on, Adam or Christian, come forward. Show us what type of man you really are when the chips are down."

She sat behind her desk and rang the hospital, saddened to hear that both Mila's and Zara's conditions had worsened overnight, but she was relieved to learn Perry had been discharged first thing.

Lunch came and went. By now, the latest appeal had aired around three times, and still no one had contacted the station with a possible sighting of Christian. Hope was dwindling fast for Sally. She had always been one of life's optimists, but the longer the day went on without any positive news coming her way, the more Sally was plunged into depression.

At around ten minutes to five, she was just finishing off the final email she had open in her inbox when the phone rang. "Hello, DI Sally Parker, how may I help?"

"It's you, isn't it? Have I got the right inspector?"

"Sorry? For what? There are numerous inspectors on duty here at the station. May I ask what this is in connection with?"

"I'm Christian Starr. Have I got the right inspector?"

Sally sat upright and flung her cup at the door to hopefully gain the attention of one of her team. Seconds later, the door opened, and a concerned Lorne stood in the opening, sporting a quizzical expression.

"Are you all right?"

Sally held her hand over the mouthpiece. "It's him. Don't shout about it, but can we get a trace done?"

Lorne's eyes widened, and she darted out of the room, closing the door gently behind her.

"That's right, Christian. I'm glad you've contacted me, I'm eager to meet up with you in person. Are you up for that?"

"Not yet. I can't trust you. I don't trust anyone."

"Why is that? Why do you feel the need to trust those around you?" she asked, trying to get an insight into how his mind worked.

"It's important to me."

"As it is to me. I can assure you, anything you say to me today will be treated with respect and complete understanding. Why don't you tell me what's going on? Why you felt the need to run from us today?"

"Because I'm misunderstood. Everything I've done the last few years was for a reason."

"And that was?" The line fell silent. She wondered if he'd

hung up on her until she detected a slight breath. "Christian, are you still there?"

"Yes, I'm choosing my words carefully, so you won't be tempted to use them against me in the future."

"Trust is a two-way street, Christian. I know you don't know me from Adam—oops, see what I did there?" Sally laughed at her unintentional faux pas, but there was still nothing from Christian's end. "Are you still with me?"

"Yes, I'm here. How is my daughter?"

"Which one?"

"Mila, of course. I know Little Fi will be fine with her mother, I would trust Laila with my life."

"And yet? You kept her in the dark about your other life, not just for a few months but for over four years. Don't you think Laila deserved to be treated better than that?"

"I was protecting her."

"From what? Or should I be asking from whom?"

Again, the silence was deafening between them.

"I can't help you if you won't confide in me, Christian," she pressed. "Why don't we meet up? You can name the time and the place. I'm willing to keep the ball in your court. The fact that you've contacted me, reached out to me, shows me how much you truly care about your family."

A sob sounded, but he quickly tried to disguise it.

Sally inhaled a steadying breath. She felt like she was teetering on a high wire, a thousand feet up, spanning across a treacherous gorge.

"I want to make amends," he whispered.

"Sorry, I didn't quite hear that. Can you repeat?"

"I said, I want to make amends... but I'm scared about the consequences."

"Doing the right thing for your family should be your priority at this stage. I rang the hospital earlier, and Mila's health is declining. They told me it's now or never, Christian.

If we delay the inevitable, it could be too late this time next week. Meet me, please?"

"I can't. I'm still coming to terms with everything. I let them all down. There's no way back from that, not in my eyes."

"Never say never. Of course there is. We'll work something out if you decide to help your family."

"I want to, believe me, but it's not that simple."

"Why? What's stopping you? What are you afraid of?"

"Letting everyone down again. What if I come in? I'll need to be tested to see if my kidneys are a match for Mila, won't I? And what happens if I'm not and she dies anyway?"

"There's only one way we're going to find out. You're going to need to put your trust in me, can you do that?"

"I don't know you or what you're capable of. I've researched, and your reputation speaks of fairness, but how do I know you won't feel different about me if we meet up, knowing that I married two women, had two families that I loved?"

"I'm willing to set my personal feelings aside for the greater good. This conversation really needs to be about Mila, nothing else should matter, not to me, and definitely not to you right now. Your daughter needs you."

"I can't. The timing isn't right."

"What timing? Your daughter's life is hanging in the balance, and only you may be able to save her now, Christian. Believe me when I say we've tried every other means available to us. None of them have worked, you're her last chance."

"What about the waiting list?"

"It's months, if not years long. The truth is, even if she lasted that long, it could still be too late. Her body might reject an organ they give her. With you coming forward, the risks will be minimal in comparison. That's why it's essential you meet with me. I can get you to the right people. Your daughter's suffering could be a thing of the past. Only you can make the right decision."

Again, silence.

"Christian? Talk to me. Tell me what's going through that mind of yours."

"You really wouldn't want to know. I've let them all down."

"You have. Coming to terms with that is the first step to putting things right. Can you tell me what yesterday was all about?"

"You mean what I did to Perry?"

"Yes. I'm still trying to figure that out."

"It's complicated."

"Try me."

"I hate the bastard, always have done. He and Julie have always treated Zara appallingly over the years. Seeing Zara in that state at the hospital tore me to shreds. I needed to get revenge, not only for myself, but for her as well. He should have been there for her... when I walked out. Instead, he made her life a misery. I've kept a close eye on Zara since I left her and Mila. Not once has he visited her at the new house. I know it was the pits and that was my fault, but where were her family when she needed them the most? Nowhere to be seen, that's where. Even her parents refused to set foot in the place. How could they disown her like that, leave her to fend for herself? You saw the results for yourself."

The irony of his words gripped her heart and squeezed it, but she was cautious about apportioning the blame in his direction. "I agree, her family failed her at the time, but I believe they've learnt their lesson and are doing the right thing for them now."

"I've only got your word on that. I saw Zara, got caught in

her room and was too scared to visit Mila on the other side of the hospital. Is someone with her? Keeping her safe through this horrendous ordeal?"

"Yes, Zara's parents are by her side. They've been amazing. They both realised their mistake early on and did the right thing immediately, were prepared to look after Mila at home, that was, until she collapsed and ended up in hospital."

"Didn't Zara know about Mila's condition? Did she neglect her?"

"I think the only thing that Zara is guilty of is neglecting herself. I honestly don't believe she had any insight as to how ill Mila was. You know what teenagers are like, they lock themselves away in their bedrooms. Zara only really saw Mila before and after school, for a fleeting moment." Sally had no idea if that scenario was an accurate one or not, but she felt the need to fight Zara's corner against the man who had temporarily forgotten that his selfish behaviour was the root cause of all that had gone on in his wife's and daughter's lives in the last two years.

"Yes, Mila has always been as independent as her mother. My biggest regret was walking out on them."

"Then why do it?"

"I had to. I didn't want them to know what a failure I was. We both put our heart and soul into the dance studio, but it was losing money from the get-go."

"Did Zara know that?"

"No, I hid the financial side of things from her."

"You tampered with the figures, to disguise the truth?"

"Yes. That's when I took out the loans."

"Didn't you consider the consequences of doing that? How did you think you were going to pay the instalments, if, as you say, the business was in trouble the minute you opened the doors?"

"I had a pipe dream that everything would turn out for

the best. Instead, it got so much worse than I had intended. I was drowning and fast, too fast, and going on the missing list was the only way I could think about getting out of it."

Sally shook her head. He hadn't thought about the consequences, not one iota. "Two wrongs don't make a right. But you can put all that behind you now and do what's necessary to change all that, Christian. Meet me."

The door eased open, and Lorne appeared. She raised a thumb and whispered that Jordan and Stuart were en route to pick him up.

Sally's gaze locked with Lorne's, and her heart raced. All she needed to do now was keep Christian talking until the boys got there.

"I can't meet you, not yet. I still have a lot of issues to work through."

"Such as? We can do that together. Where are you?"

"No, it's no good you trying to trick me."

"I'm not, that's the furthest thing from my mind. Name the time and the place and I'll be there."

The line fell quiet once more, and Sally closed her eyes. *Fuck, have I messed things up? Am I trying too hard?*

Lorne jotted down something on a notebook and slid it in front of Sally. She read the message, shook her head and mouthed, "I can't tell him that, he'll freak out." But it didn't stop Sally mulling over the suggestion one more time.

Lorne nodded. "Do it."

"Christian, how would you feel about speaking with Laila?"

"What? When? Is this a trick?"

"No, she's here, with us, at the station. Come and see her. I can tell Little Fi is missing her dad." He swallowed, then cleared his throat. "Christian, don't walk away from them, too, they need you."

"But I've lied to her. She won't want to be with me again, not after she knows the truth."

"You're wrong. She does. You obviously heard what Laila had to say during the appeal. The only thing she wants from you is for you to do the right thing by Mila. She's desperate, Christian. Won't you reconsider coming to the station? Your family are here waiting for you."

"No, she's just saying that. I know Laila of old, she's not the forgiving type."

His comment shocked her. Sally ran a shaking hand around her face, the pressure getting to her now, which was daft. She'd never found herself in such an untenable situation before, in all her years on the Force. Lorne lowered her hands, intimating for Sally to keep calm.

"Nothing could be further from the truth. She's here, waiting for you, eager to see you."

Suddenly, a man called out Christian Starr's name. She recognised the voice as Jordan's.

"Those are my men, they've come to collect you, Christian. Don't run, they'll use Tasers if they have to this time."

He groaned and disconnected the call.

"Shit! He hung up on me." She picked up her mobile and called Jordan's number. It rang several times before a breathless Jordan answered. "Have you got him? Tell me you have."

"We've got him, boss. We're bringing him in now."

"Great job. See you when you get here." She ended the call, threw her phone on the desk, and she flung herself back in her chair. "Thank God for that, they've got him. It's about time."

Lorne beamed. "Congratulations, you pulled a blinder, Sally Parker. I'm so proud of you."

"Get away with you. Just because we've picked him up it doesn't end there. Next on the agenda is the tiny matter of trying to persuade him to hand over one of his kidneys."

Lorne grimaced. "Rather you than me. That's going to take some doing, but if anyone can do it, you can."

"You do talk out of your arse at times."

"Are you going to break the news to Laila, or do you want me to?"

"I'll come and do it. How are they both doing out there?"

"She's a good mum. It's been a breeze for her, no stress from what I can tell, caring for Little Fi."

"I wouldn't have expected anything less from her. She must be shellshocked by what she's been confronted with today."

"I wonder what her reaction is going to be, once she hears the news."

Sally left her chair and walked towards Lorne. "Let's find out."

Laila stared at them as they approached her. "What's wrong?"

Sally picked up on the trepidation in Laila's tone. "We've got him. He's unharmed and on his way here."

The young woman reached for her daughter, who was merrily playing with her teddy, and held her tightly. "Thank God. What will happen next?"

"Well, I would suggest that you go home now that we know he's been caught. We'll keep him here for the night, we're going to need to question him. I don't think that will take long; he was reasonably talkative on the phone."

"I see. How will I get home?"

Sally faced Lorne and asked, "Are you up for it?"

"Of course. I'll help you pack up your stuff and we'll get on the road."

"Thank you. You have all been amazing. I've always been afraid of the police, don't ask me why, in-built fear as a child, I suppose. But you've showed me nothing but kindness since I met you."

"At the end of the day, we're just ordinary people, carrying out our jobs, serving the public."

Laila smiled. "I bet not everyone at this station is as kind as you are."

Sally smiled. "No comment."

LAILA, the baby and Lorne had gone by the time Jordan and Stuart returned with Christian.

Sally couldn't wait to get started with the interview, even though it was nearing six and at the end of their shift. "Are you up for sitting in with me, Stuart?"

"Me? Yes, I'd love to, boss. Let me grab a fresh notebook."

"Right, let's see what the man has to say for himself. Did he talk much in the car?"

"Not really, he just stared out of the window," Stuart replied.

STUART SAID the necessary verbiage for the recording. Sally spent the time observing the suspect. Her initial assessment, without him saying a word, was that he appeared to be a broken man.

"For the purpose of this interview, I'm going to be calling you Christian, is that all right with you?"

He shrugged. "Whatever. Why am I here? You tricked me, I knew you would."

"I didn't, not in the slightest. You refused to tell me where you were. I asked you numerous times to meet me, and you wouldn't, therefore, I had to take matters into my own hands. All of this could have been avoided if only you had trusted me."

"I don't trust anyone, I told you that over the phone. Where's my wife?"

"Which one?"

"Laila, you told me she was here, with Little Fi. I want to see them."

"They were here. As soon as you were taken into custody, she asked to leave. My partner has taken them home. Why put them through all of this, Christian?"

He squirmed and wrung his hands. "I didn't, not knowingly."

"Not knowingly? You've been with Laila for four years. She only knows you as Adam Henson. The deception was cast in stone when you met, wasn't it?"

"No. Yes. Oh, I don't know. It seemed a good idea at the time, to introduce myself as someone new. It felt good to leave my troubles behind when I was with her."

"Are you telling me that the dishonesty and lies sat well with you?"

"I wouldn't say that. My life was hell when I was with Zara, she wanted the best of everything, and I felt inadequate most of the time."

"That's why you took out the loans?"

"Yes, it seemed to be an answer to our problems. But she wanted more and more."

"Why? Because you misled her, told her the business was doing well when it had been leaking money from day one?"

His head dipped to avoid eye contact with her.

"Don't you think she deserved more than that?" Sally prompted.

"Yes. It was one of those ideas that got out of hand quickly. I regret my actions, you have to believe me."

"Do you? Enough to give up a kidney for your daughter?"

His head shot up again. "I... I'm not sure if I could go through that."

Sally sat back and folded her arms. "Would you mind telling me what the alternative is? I mean, I know what it is, having spoken to the consultant at the hospital. Clearly, you have a different idea, so what is it?"

His gaze shifted between them and then dropped to the floor beside him.

"You can't give me an answer because I believe you think your daughter will be strong enough to pull through this, don't you?"

"She's always been strong, just like her mother. Both women in my life have the same qualities, that's why I love them."

"We're veering off track here. We were talking about Mila. Do you believe she will recover after a few days' rest in hospital?"

"Doesn't everyone?"

"No, that's simply not true, not without some form of intervention from the doctors. I can't emphasise enough just how sick your daughter is. But you have the ability to help her."

"How? By giving up one of my vital organs? I know I have two kidneys, but what if the other one stops functioning, what then?"

"That's the risk most people are willing to take if it means saving the life of a loved one."

He covered his eyes with his hand and rubbed at them. "You're effectively asking me to sign my own death certificate in advance."

"That's nonsense. Why are you making this all about you when it's your daughter's welfare that should be your first and only priority?"

Christian sat there, his thoughts clearly racing, until he said, "I need to see her before I decide."

Even though Sally was shocked by his statement, she smiled and nodded. "Of course, we can arrange for you to see her."

"Now?"

"I'll have to see if she's up to it. I've rung the hospital a few times today, and each time they've told me that she's getting worse and needs to rest."

"Shit! Is she really that bad?"

She resisted the temptation to roll her eyes. "She truly is. I'm not in the habit of telling people their loved ones are on the brink of death just for the sake of it. Get a good night's sleep, and I'll make the call to visit Mila first thing in the morning, how's that?"

It took him a while of soul-searching before he finally sat back and whispered, "Yes, I'd like to see her. Can we end this here, now? I'm tired, it's been a hectic couple of days."

"If that's what you want. We can continue the interview after we've visited Mila tomorrow."

Stuart ended the recording and led Christian to his cell.

Sally returned to the office to find Lorne already there. "How did it go with Laila?"

"She was quiet on the journey back but appreciative of us keeping her in the loop. What about Christian? Did you learn anything new?"

"Only that he appears to be reluctant about supplying his daughter with the kidney she needs to survive. He's asked to see her. I've told him we'll go first thing and complete the interview afterwards."

"Let's hope he does the right thing by his daughter, but I'm not so sure."

"Me, too. I guess people's selfish behaviour will never cease to amaze me. I'm dead on my feet. Well done, guys. Let's go home and start afresh in the morning."

## CHAPTER 11

The next morning, Christian told them that he'd had a rough night but was eager to see Mila. Sally drove to Norwich hospital at nine-fifteen. When they reached Mila's room, Sally and Lorne had to act as referees between Christian and Zara's parents.

"Listen, you lot having a go at each other isn't going to help, is it? You need to put your anger aside and do what's best for Mila," Sally insisted.

"*He needs* to do what's right for Mila." Leslie Walters jabbed a finger in Christian's chest.

"That's enough, Les. We need to listen to the inspector. It's good to see you, Christian. Please consider what this will mean to Mila. She's not well at all, you'll see that for yourself. We'll get a drink in the canteen. You can find us there," Amy Walters said. She pushed her husband in the back all the way down the hallway.

Christian paced the area immediately outside Mila's room. "I'm not sure I can do this."

Sally clutched his arm. "We'll be right beside you, just see how you go. Are you ready?"

He nodded and expelled a long-suffering breath. "I think so."

Sally led the way into the room. Christian followed, and Lorne brought up the rear and remained by the door just in case Christian decided to bolt, shirking his responsibilities.

He approached the bed. His daughter's cheeks were pale and her brow knitted as if she were in constant pain. Sally observed the changing expressions on Christian's face.

He swept back a stray hair from Mila's right eye and bent to kiss her. "My dear, sweet child. How has it come to this? Can you hear me?"

The door opened, and the doctor entered. "Ah, you're here. As you can see, Mila is really suffering now."

"What does that mean, Doctor?" Sally asked.

"She's going downhill rapidly. If we don't find a donor soon... well, it'll probably be too late. We've got her on strong pain relief but fear it's not enough. Have you considered doing the test?" he asked Christian.

"I... I don't think I could give away one of my organs, I'm sorry."

The doctor raised an eyebrow, and his eyes narrowed. "That's entirely your prerogative, but as you can see for yourself, your daughter's condition isn't improving, and it's only going to get worse before the inevitable happens."

Christian stared at Mila. He ran a hand around her face and bent low to whisper something in her ear. Sally was too far away to make out what he'd said.

"Christian, listen to the doctor, please. If we don't act soon, it'll be too late. Could you go through the rest of your life, knowing that one selfless act from yourself could have given your daughter the means to live her life to a ripe old age?"

He stood erect and stared at Sally. "That's easy for you to say, it's my life that will be changed forever."

"Actually, it will change both your lives, your daughter's significantly for the better. I could have the operating theatre ready for action within half an hour, you only have to say the word."

Christian left his daughter's bedside and paced the floor between everyone else in the room. "You're asking a lot of me. I'm not sure I'm prepared to give up an organ... not yet."

The doctor sighed. "Then you might as well say goodbye to Mila, because she isn't going to last long."

"This is emotional blackmail," Christian shouted.

"Keep your voice down," the doctor warned. "Actually, I've had enough. I can tell your daughter means nothing to you. You being here is only going to cause her more stress. I must insist that you leave."

Sally stepped towards Christian and placed a hand on his forearm. "Don't give up the chance to make a huge difference to your daughter's life. She needs you."

He shook his head. "I'm scared... scared to do the right thing."

The doctor stepped forward. "I can sit you down and go through the process step by step, if that's what you want. There truly isn't anything to worry about. We're experienced in this field, nothing is taken lightly, everything is always carefully considered. All we want to do is what's right for your daughter."

"I want that, too. I'm eager to make up for the mistakes I have made in the past, to rectify things between us, but... I think this is one step too far."

"Please, Christian, put yourself in her shoes at this age. If you'd needed a kidney to survive, what would your parents have done?"

"They weren't as selfish as me," he shot back without hesitation. He crossed the room, his gaze drawn to his daughter.

Sally stared at Lorne, unsure what to say next. Lorne shrugged, unable to supply any other suggestions that might sway him into making the right decision.

After several fraught, silent minutes, Christian stopped walking and stared at his daughter. "Okay, I'll do it."

Sally closed her eyes, relief flooding through her.

The doctor smiled. "You've made the right decision. I'll arrange for the test to be carried out and ensure the operating staff are put on standby."

Two hours later, they received the results from the test which proved Christian was a match. Sally noticed he didn't seem as scared now.

"The theatres are set up, we're good to go," the doctor told them a little while later. "If you'd like to come with me, we'll get you ready for the operation."

Sally and Lorne accompanied them, just in case Christian was trying to trick them into thinking he was doing the right thing and intended to take off at the first chance that came his way. Outside the room, Mila's grandparents rose from their chairs.

"Any news?" Amy asked, her eyes welling up with tears.

"Yes, Mr Starr has agreed to go through with the operation," the doctor informed her.

Amy sank into her chair and sobbed. "Thank you… thank you… thank you."

Leslie hugged his wife and glanced up at Christian. "We will never be able to thank you enough for this."

Christian smiled, and they all set off down the long corridor. The doctor explained that the operation could take between three and four hours. Sally told him that they would wait until Christian and Mila were back in recovery.

The wait turned out to be longer than anticipated. During

the operation, Sally and Lorne spent some of the time sitting with Zara, reassuring her that everything was going to be all right. Zara looked as if a huge weight had been lifted from her shoulders. There was a brightness in her eyes that had been missing before.

"I'm glad he's doing the right thing… at last. Has he shown any remorse for his sins?"

Sally smiled. "Not verbally, but you can see it in his features. It took a lot of persuading to get him into the theatre. Let's hope this is a new beginning for all of you."

"I'm not sure what lies ahead for either of us, but I'll be forever grateful to him for putting Mila first, when it mattered."

# EPILOGUE

Sally and Lorne remained at the hospital all day, flitting between the rooms of the three patients, Zara, Mila and Christian. At around six, Stuart and Jordan joined them. Sally had asked them to pick up Laila and bring her to the hospital so that she could be with her husband. Little Fi had remained at home with Laila's close friend.

"Hello, Laila, how are you?" Sally asked when they'd met up outside Christian's room.

"I'm eager to see Adam, shit, or should I be calling him Christian?"

"I think we'll stick with Christian, if it's all the same with you?"

"Whatever. Can I see him now?"

"Yes. The last time I checked he was just coming around. Don't be surprised if he's dropped off to sleep again, he's gone through a major operation." Sally opened the door and led the way.

Laila hesitantly put one foot in front of the other and approached her husband. She touched his face, and his eyes flicked open. He smiled and held up a hand for her to hold.

"You came. I thought I'd lost you," he whispered.

Sally smiled, happy to see the couple reunited. "I'll be outside. Don't be too long, he needs his rest."

"I won't." Laila sat in the chair alongside her husband, and Sally left the room.

She sat next to Lorne who was almost dropping off in her seat. "It's been a long day, no, make it a long week. The weekend is just around the corner, something to look forward to."

"Definitely. I'm tempted to go away for a few days, but that's not likely to happen, is it? Not with the dogs to care for."

"Get your manager to put in a couple of extra shifts for you."

"No, something like this needs careful planning. I'll put it on hold for a few days. How did the reunion go?"

"It went well. He was pleased to see her. Laila was a tad hesitant to begin with, but it was all good in the end. We'll give them half an hour and then interrupt them. Boys, if you want to head home, that's fine by me. We can drop Laila off on the way through."

Stuart and Jordan both rose from their seats. "If you're sure, boss?" Stuart asked.

A nurse walked past them and opened the door to Christian's room.

"Go before I change my mind," Sally ordered.

The nurse screamed and dropped the metal dish she was holding.

Stuart was the first to react. He ran into the room and shouted, "Fuck. Get away from him."

Fearing the worst, Sally bolted after him and stood frozen to the spot when she saw Laila standing there with a bloody kitchen knife in her hand.

"Come near me and I'll kill myself," Laila warned.

Stuart withdrew his Taser and yelled, "Drop the weapon or I'll fire."

Sally was in a daze, completely bewildered by what was taking place before her tired eyes. Her gaze drifted to the bed. Christian's pillow was covered in blood from the huge wound in his throat. His eyes were wide open, staring at the ceiling. "Why, Laila? How could you?"

"How could I? He was a liar and a cheat. Yes, he did the right thing by his daughter in the end but look at the stress he's caused us all. He was a selfish bastard to Zara, and to me. I couldn't bear the thought of him going back to her, leaving Little Fi and me to cope on our own."

"So you killed him?"

"Drop the knife," Stuart warned again.

She failed to comply with his command, so he fired the trigger.

The knife slid under the bed, and Laila slumped on the floor, propped up against the wall until Stuart and Jordan removed the wires and slapped the cuffs on her.

On the verge of vomiting, Sally shouted, "Get her out of my sight."

Lorne rushed to comfort Sally. "Are you all right?"

Tears of anger mixed with frustration and guilt emerged. "Why did I leave her alone with him? I should have realised something like this might happen."

"Sal, listen to me, you can't blame yourself."

"Can't I?" Sally covered her face with her hands and sobbed.

Lorne hugged her, stroked her back and whispered, "None of this is your fault. The family were screwed up already, all of them. You made all the right moves. I backed you fully in every decision you made. Come on, dry those tears. Let's get you home."

. . .

THE END

Thank you for reading COPING WITHOUT YOU. The next book in this exciting cold case series **Could It Be Him?**

In the meantime, have you read any of my other fast paced crime thrillers yet? Why not try the first book in the DI Sara Ramsey series No Right to Kill

Or grab the first book in the bestselling, award-winning, Justice series here, Cruel Justice.

Or the first book in the spin-off Justice Again series, Gone In Seconds.

Why not try the first book in the DI Sam Cobbs series, set in the beautiful Lake District, To Die For.

Perhaps you'd prefer to try one of my other police procedural series, the DI Kayli Bright series which begins with The Missing Children.

Or maybe you'd enjoy the DI Sally Parker series set in Norfolk, Wrong Place.

. . .

M A COMLEY

Or my gritty police procedural starring DI Nelson set in Manchester, Torn Apart.

Or maybe you'd like to try one of my successful psychological thrillers She's Gone, I KNOW THE TRUTH or Shattered Lives.

# KEEP IN TOUCH WITH M A COMLEY

Pick up a FREE novella by signing up to my newsletter today.
https://BookHip.com/WBRTGW

BookBub
www.bookbub.com/authors/m-a-comley

Blog

http://melcomley.blogspot.com

Why not join my special Facebook group to take part in monthly giveaways.

Readers' Group

Printed in Great Britain
by Amazon